4/05

A SURPRISE
FOR ABIGAIL

A SURPRISE
FOR ABIGAIL

•

Tracey J. Lyons

AVALON BOOKS
NEW YORK

PRINTED IN THE UNITED STATES OF AMERICA
ON ACID-FREE PAPER
BY HADDON CRAFTSMEN, BLOOMSBURG, PENNSYLVANIA

This one is for my mom.
Happy Birthday!

Chapter One

Catskill Mountains
Surprise, New York
1882

"Is he dead?"

"I don't know. Poke him and see if he moves."

Cole Stanton lay on his back with one arm flung out to the side and the other laying across his forehead, shielding his eyes from the blinding daylight. Painfully, he raised one eyelid, catching a glimpse of two boys—one with dark curly hair, the other a freckle-faced blond—standing outside his jail cell. Even that small movement proved to be too much. He snapped his eye shut, listening as two sets of feet shuffled around the room.

1

Whatever instrument of torture the boys had found to poke him with scraped against the metal bars of his jail cell. The noise was deafening and he was sure his eardrums were going to break. He held his breath, waiting for the jab. He felt a sharp stab to his rib cage and rolled off the cot, onto the floor, landing on his back.

At the sight of him laying face up, staring at them, the boys dropped the stick and ran screaming from the jail. If his head wasn't about to explode, Cole would have enjoyed a good laugh at their expense. As it was, he lay there wondering how he was going to get himself up from the floor. His mouth tasted like a stale cigar and his ears were filled with, what sounded like, the buzzing of a thousand locusts.

The worst of it was, though, he couldn't remember where he was or how he'd gotten here. He recognized the bars of a jail cell and knew that the pain came from a grand hangover, but try as he may, Cole couldn't remember what town he was in.

There was a vague recollection of being on a train and reaching for his bags only to realize they'd been stolen right out from underneath him. Literally. When he'd boarded the train he'd tucked the travel bag under his seat for safekeeping. Now he was thankful that he'd had the sense enough to leave most of his life savings in the bank because the thief would have stolen that too.

Hearing the door to the sheriff's office open, he winced, the pain in his head moving behind his eyes. Groaning, he hoped whoever it was walking through the door was coming to put him out of his misery, or bringing him some water.

Damn, he sure was thirsty.

"The sheriff will be along in a minute."

Cole squinted up through a blurry haze at the man leaning against the bars. Unruly brown hair framed a thin face, and light brown eyes peered at him from beneath a set of thick bushy eyebrows. Dressed in dark pants and a matching jacket, Cole would have thought him to be the lawman.

"Water." Barely managing to rasp the word out, he wasn't sure the man heard him.

"Water!"

"Yeah, I heard what you said, Mister. I'll give you some water, but only if you promise you're not going to throw it back up. The sheriff wouldn't take too kindly to having the jail cell dirtied up by some drunken stranger."

The kind soul walked away from Cole mumbling, "Only got the place back into tip-top shape just last week. Wouldn't be right if somebody messed it up so soon."

By the time the gentleman had poured the water into the tin cup, Cole had managed to push himself up into a sitting position, resting his back against the wall next to the cot.

"I'm not going to retch."

Returning to the cell, the man put the cup in Cole's outstretched hand. "That's good to hear." Squatting down, with the bars between them, he asked, "What's your name?"

He stopped gulping the cool water long enough to answer, "Cole Stanton."

"I'd take care not to drink that so fast, if I were you."

Ignoring his concern, Cole emptied the cup and held it out for some more. He sat up a little straighter and opened both eyes, taking in his surroundings. The cell he'd spent the night in was tiny, barely big enough to hold him and the narrow cot.

He looked over to where the man was pouring his second cup of water—he was shadowed by an entry flanked by two long, narrow windows. A large desk sat square in the room. A map of the States hung on the white-washed lathe and plaster wall behind it. As his senses slowly began to return, Cole noticed the aroma.

The scent was from his past, reminding him of warm summer rain and sunshine; of a happier time in his life. It was a part of his life that had been locked away in the back of his mind and in his heart for a long time. He closed his eyes, shuttering away the memory. Opening his eyes wider, he saw the small vase filled with white Lillies of the Valley sitting on one corner of the desk.

The sheriff must have a wife or a sweetheart, someone with a tender side who thought that the flowers would brighten the room. Or someone who wanted to leave a reminder so her man couldn't forget her.

The man brought back the cup and handed it through the bars to him. "You got a name?" Cole asked.

"John Wagner."

"Nice to meet you, John Wagner." He handed the cup back through the bars.

"You want more?"

"No, two's enough for now." He'd wished he'd had that attitude last night when he'd been drinking himself half-blind.

"You might want to straighten yourself up a bit, the sheriff will be around in a minute."

"Yeah, I'll get right on it," Cole muttered.

He was standing, testing out his balance, when the entry door opened. A young, dark-haired woman entered. Resting against the bars, he stared at her. There was something about the curve of her mouth and the piercing gaze coming from those hazel eyes that pricked at the edges of his memory.

For a frightening moment he wondered if he'd made a pass at her last night and had no recollection of it, and now she'd come to seek revenge for her lost virtue. Then he looked her over and almost laughed—she wasn't his type. Oh, her curves were in all the right places, it's just that they were all covered up with an ugly brown dress.

"Good morning, Mr. Wagner."

"Morning, Sheriff."

Sheriff! That snip of a thing was the sheriff? Cole leaned his forehead against the cold steel bars, moaning in disbelief.

"Is everything all right, sir?" Mr. Wagner asked.

"Where am I?" Cole demanded.

"Why you're in jail."

"I know that, I mean what's the name of this town?"

"Surprise!" Mr. Wagner puffed out his chest as he made the proclamation.

Cole raised his head and stared at the two people who stood several feet away from him. They had to be crazy. "I don't need anymore surprises! Just tell me where I am," he shouted.

"Now see here, Mister, there's no need for you to be yelling and cussing."

Mr. Wagner sure was right about that one. Cole winced as pain shot across his right temple. When the pain subsided, he managed to mumble an apology. "Sorry. Just tell me where I am."

"Mr. Wagner already did that, sir. You are in the town of Surprise."

Her voice was so soft, like silk. Closing his eyes, he concentrated on the memory of it. Last night— it had to be her—she'd spoken to him last night.

Opening his eyes, he looked at her. The same hazel eyes and midnight-black hair that he remembered. Except, her hair looked much better this morning. He smiled as the memory became clearer.

She ran a hand over her hair, and then smoothed down the folds of her brown skirt. "Is there a problem?" She looked at him, her gaze fierce and unwavering.

"I say, you look a might better this morning, ma'am," Cole taunted.

"I wish that the same could be said for you, sir," she retorted.

He almost laughed, but the words stung. Cole was well aware of how he appeared. For years he'd been moving from town to town picking up odd jobs. This last time he'd even hung around long enough to set up a business as a contractor. His gaze dropped to his callused hands; there was nothing like the satisfaction of building things with your own two hands.

But then the memories caught up with him and it was time to run again. A person would think that after all this time he'd have come to realize that you can't run from yourself. Turning his head towards the wall, he caught a glimpse of himself in the piece of broken mirror that hung lopsided on the brick. A rough looking character stared back at him.

His face was covered with a dark full beard and he'd stopped caring about the length of his hair three towns ago. He didn't want to look into the dirt brown eyes that stared back at him. Cole remembered a clean-shaven face, short clipped hair, and eyes that weren't so filled with the bitter truth of the world. Blinking hard he cleared away the image.

He'd learned the hard way that once innocence was gone a person could never reclaim it.

"Mr. Wagner will take you to the—the necessary."

Cole turned at the sound of her voice, grinning when he saw the blush spreading across her pretty face. The barred door swung open and Cole walked out of the cell. She'd turned her back to him.

"There's some fresh towels and soap." With a wave of her hand she indicated a small pile on the corner of her desk. "You'll find some rain water in the barrel out back."

As soon as the back door shut, Abigail collapsed onto the chair behind the desk. Placing her elbows on the desktop, she rested her chin on the palms of her hands.

This prisoner was turning out to be more than she bargained for when she'd agreed to do this job.

Oh, but why, of all things about last night, had he remembered the way she looked? The thought made her want to crawl under the desk and never come out. She'd just fallen into a deep sleep when the pounding on the door started and there'd been no time to fix herself up properly, not with Mr. Jules hurrying her along.

She'd followed as he led the way down the street to the small saloon, her pulse still racing from being awakened from a sound sleep.

Raucous laughter, bawdy singing and the smell of stale beer greeted them when they arrived. "Right through here, Miss, sir, I mean, Sheriff."

Her loose hair had brushed against her shoulders as they'd stumbled through the narrow doorway. She remembered pushing a hank of hair wrapped in the cloth strip off her forehead, tucking the lock under her bonnet to get a better view of what the commotion was all about. Standing behind Mr. Jules, she'd peered around his shoulder, wishing she'd had a gun.

Abigail remembered thinking if she'd been brandishing a gun, none of the rest of the events would have happened. Abigail was certain of that. A gun made the man or in her case *would* make the woman. It was pretty hard to laugh at someone when they had a gun pointed at you.

Unfortunately she hadn't been able to convince the ridiculous town council to let her carry one. When she argued with them, they were quick to point out that the former sheriff, Chauncy, didn't feel the need to have one therefore she shouldn't either. They wanted to believe that this town was safe, and indeed it was. However, she was the sheriff and as such should be allowed to have a gun.

Perched precariously on a bar stool, sat Mr. Cole Stanton. A half-empty glass of liquor was swinging back and forth in his unsteady hand. Every so often the liquid would swish around spilling over the rim. The scarred pine bar and his pants were puddled with the drink.

Abruptly, Mr. Jules had stepped to the right, exposing Abigail. As the patrons began to notice her, a hush fell over the room. Mr. Stanton stopped singing, gaping at her. And then he'd tipped his head back and laughed. The rich booming sound had filled her ears, making her mad. She was the Sheriff and should be shown some respect. What right did he have to mock her?

Then she'd caught sight of herself in the bar mirror. There was no doubt about it; a male sheriff wouldn't have been caught dead looking the way she did!

Her stomach fluttered in nausea as she remembered. Rag curls were sticking out from underneath her bonnet and the dress that she'd managed to get into was buttoned so that she'd placed the second button in the fourth button hole.

Thankfully, she'd remembered most of her unmentionables and had even managed to grab the sheriff's badge off the night stand, but in her haste she'd pinned it to her dress upside-down.

Groaning, she came back to the present and, pressing the heels of her hands to her eyes, thought that last night had been the most humiliating moment in her entire *new* life, a life that was supposed to be better than her old one. In that life she'd been jilted by her betrothed of two months, Edwin Quinn. He'd told her it was because he wasn't ready for marriage, and yet four weeks to the day they'd broken off their engagement, he'd gone and married Jennifer Matthews.

Jennifer was everything Abigail wasn't; a bright, vivacious young woman with blond hair and sky-blue eyes. Abigail had always been a bit shy and saw herself as ordinary in comparison. Edwin had tried to console her breaking heart by telling her that this shouldn't have come as any surprise. For Abigail it had been the most painful of surprises.

Right then and there she'd decided there would be no more surprises in her life. Abigail Monroe was going to take control and one thing was for certain, she wouldn't be falling in love again anytime soon.

She blew out a long frustrated sigh not even sure she knew how to take control of her life, but she was certainly going to give the idea a go.

The back door opened, shaking her out of her

ponderings. She swiveled the chair around to face the door. Mr. Stanton had washed up, tucked in his shirt and even managed to straighten his hair. The humiliation of last night still fresh in her mind, she avoided meeting his dark gaze.

"Thank you kindly for letting me use your facilities. If you don't mind my asking, am I free to go?"

"No. Your punishment hasn't been decided." Abigail glanced at Mr. Wagner, waiting for him to contradict her as he seemed to be so wanting to do. Of all the people in this town she'd yet to convince Aunt Margaret's adviser that she was capable of doing this job.

He wiggled his thick graying eyebrows at her in that annoying way he had and said, "Today is Sunday."

"And . . . ?" she asked, and then she remembered. "Ah, yes, silly me. How could I have forgotten? Mr. Stanton, you're about to learn about the Founding Father's rule, or in this case, the Founding Mother's rule: No prisoner shall eat Sunday dinner in jail."

Abigail quickly followed with her feelings about this little tradition. "Of course the notion is so ridiculous."

"I don't know about that, ma'am. I kind of like the idea of having a nice Sunday dinner." Mr. Stanton grinned.

"Mr. Stanton, could you kindly stop referring to me as *ma'am?*"

"What would you like me to call you, sir?" Cole chuckled.

"Sheriff Abigail," she replied. Since her swearing-in a month ago, everyone had taken to calling her that, so she didn't see any reason why this criminal, as she'd taken to thinking of him, shouldn't call her that too.

"Mr. Wagner, please tell Mr. Stanton where he is having dinner."

"Mrs. Margaret Monroe Sinclair is expecting us."

Chapter Two

"Who is this Margaret Monroe Sinclair?" Cole asked.

"My aunt," Abigail answered, following the men to the door.

As the trio left the building two boys darted in front of them. Using her best authoritative voice, Abigail scolded the youngsters. "James Macintyre and Matthew Duncan, it isn't polite to rush out in front of people like that."

The boys stopped in their tracks and turned to face her. They stared at her, their eyes widening with fear. She couldn't help thinking that perhaps she'd spoken a little too harshly. She was about to apologize when she followed the direction of their stare—to Cole Stanton.

14

His eyes were narrowed into slits, as he stared in a positively dark, sinister way at the duo.

"Boys, do you know this man?"

"No, no, we don't, Sheriff Abigail. We ain't never seen him before have we, Matt?" James poked his friend in the ribs. His freckled face went white as a sheet.

"No. No sirree. I mean, ma'am," Matthew corrected quickly, shaking a head full of dark curls.

"Run along, now." The two tore out of there like the devil himself was chasing after them. "Now, what do you suppose got into them?" Abigail asked.

"Looks to me like Mr. Stanton here has scared the wits out of them," Mr. Wagner answered with a chuckle.

Continuing their walk to Aunt Margaret's, Abigail stole a glance at Mr. Stanton, noting several things. While Mr. Wagner stood four or so inches taller than she, Mr. Stanton positively dwarfed them. His face was covered by a thick brown whiskered beard. All she could see were his nose, dark whiskey-brown eyes, a patch of pale skin on his forehead and around his mouth.

She wondered what all that hair was covering up? Before she knew what was happening, Mr. Stanton caught her studying him. As his dark gaze fixed upon hers, his full lips turned up into a wicked smile, showing two fine rows of white teeth.

Never in her life had a man looked at her like

that; as if he was going to devour her one bite at a time. She felt the heat of a blush spreading up her neck and across her face. Feeling her new-found confidence suddenly on very shaky ground, Abigail straightened her spine.

It was hard for her to forget just how reserved she'd once been; how easily she'd let herself be led into doing other's bidding. That had all changed when Edwin left her for another woman. He'd actually done her a great favor, his deceit spurring her on, forcing her to become braver.

Tired of letting life pass her by, Abigail had grabbed life by the horns, jumping at the chance to come stay with Aunt Margaret—thinking a change of scenery was just the balm she needed. Now, just as she was feeling like she could do anything, Mister Cole Stanton was trying his best to intimidate her with just one look.

She wasn't going to be having any of this man's nonsense.

"Howdy, Miss. Nice to see you, sir," Stanton said as he nodded his head and greeted every single person they passed.

Abigail was infuriated with him. "Stop that right now."

"Stop what?"

"Being so nice to everyone. You are supposed to be getting your punishment for drunken behavior. The least you could do is act a little remorseful."

He slighted her with a dark glance. "Are you serious?"

"Of course I am. I'm the sheriff and drunken disorderly behavior is a serious offense!" If she hadn't been trying so hard to keep up with the long strides of the two men, she'd have stopped to stamp her foot for proper emphasis.

"That it is. But I'm not sitting in a jail cell right now, am I?"

"No. But if I had my way, you'd still be there," Abigail mumbled.

"I don't doubt it." He'd heard her words. "But you wouldn't want me to be looking mean and crazy, scaring your townsfolk on my way to Sunday dinner now, would you?"

Abigail rolled her eyes heavenward. This whole situation had been crazy from the very moment she'd arrived in town. She'd come here because her aunt was sick. Then she'd found herself talked into filling in as the sheriff. Abigail had to keep reminding herself that this was a new, braver life.

However, never in her wildest imaginings would she have seen herself walking down the main street of Surprise with her aunt's adviser and a common criminal keeping her company, on their way to Sunday dinner of all things.

"No, I don't want you worrying my neighbors," she finally admitted.

There were plenty of other things to worry about.

Such as fulfilling her duties as sheriff and making sure that Aunt Margaret was being taken care of properly.

She was content to continue what she'd been doing for the past month while mending her broken heart; worrying on her own and keeping Surprise what it had always been, a sleepy little town. *A place where nothing out of the ordinary ever happened.*

The town still had the same dusty road, a general store, post office, church, a small livery and one boarding house. Walking past the old saw mill, she couldn't help feeling a little sad at the dilapidated appearance of the structure. The building looked as if it hadn't been used in years. There was a cluster of homes at one end of town with the railroad bordering the other.

Surprise, a town aptly named, seemed to appear out of nowhere. One minute you were riding along through the rolling fields and the next you were in the town. And just as quickly the buildings and street ended.

The centerpiece of the hamlet, according to Aunt Margaret, was *her* home. The grandest dwelling was made up of square-cut native rubblestone, with a hyphen hallway that connected the structure to the larger two-story clapboard addition. This house was her aunt's pride and joy; a place where Abigail had spent many lazy summers playing on the lawn with her two cousins, Lydia and Maggie.

As she led her prisoner up the wide porch steps, Abigail wished her cousins were here. At three years her senior, Lydia was the one who was full of life. She could be counted on to act first and think about the consequences later—much later.

And Margaret, her junior by just six months, was the sensible one, always doing what was best for everyone involved. Abigail was the one in the middle. She'd been the shadow who'd followed in the wake of Lydia and stood in awe of Maggie's calm command of any situation.

Stepping onto the claret-colored carpet partially covering the dark wood floor of the foyer, she caught the familiar scent of lavender potpourri. She knew the blue urn on the entryway table was filled with it. The smell had an instantaneous affect, settling around her like a warm blanket. The long hallway was laden with dark furniture, and ornately framed family portraits graced the white painted walls.

The meticulously decorated sprawling three-story home was a vivid contrast to the stark simplicity of the town. And she loved it. Standing next to her, Mr. Stanton elicited a low whistle, interrupting her feeling of contentment.

"This is some place."

"This is my aunt's home. You would do well to remember your manners, Mr. Stanton." Steeling a glance at him from the corner of her eye, Abigail doubted this man had any manners. And if he did, they certainly had been left by the roadside a long time ago.

From the far recesses of the house came the sound of a bell ringing.

"Ah, she knows we've arrived." Mr. Wagner motioned for them to follow.

They walked through the long hallway and entered the dining room. This room was done as was the rest of the house, with rich details. The focal point of the room, a portrait of Abigail and her two cousins sitting at their aunt's feet, hung on the cream-colored wall over the fireplace mantel.

Her aunt was seated at the far end of the long cherry-planked dining table, the large wicker wheelchair dwarfing her small frame. She sat bundled amidst a collection of woolen blankets. "My guests at last!" A frail hand appeared from beneath the mound of cloth, gesturing, beckoning them to come into the room.

"Good afternoon, Aunt." Leaving Mr. Stanton standing in the doorway, Abigail dutifully dropped a kiss on her aunt's pale cheek. Shock still rolled through her whenever she saw her aunt. It was hard to get used to her sickly appearance.

Her aunt had had dark chestnut-colored hair and

a round face that always had a rosy glow. This woman's hair was gray, and hadn't a dark strand in it. Her face, drawn and wrinkled, was a ghostly pasty white.

Abigail's first thought upon seeing Aunt Margaret weeks ago was that she was dying and she'd arrived just in time to say a final good-bye.

It was hard to forget the panic that had welled up inside of her when she'd first seen her aunt. Was this the same woman who'd played at three-legged races with her three young nieces? But today her aunt was here in the dining room holding court like a queen; an encouraging sign that surely her health was on the mend.

Glancing towards the doorway, Aunt Margaret said, "I see you've brought our dinner guest."

Abigail frowned down at her. "Aunt, please remember he is not a guest, Mr. Stanton is my prisoner."

"That's right, silly me, I forgot." Raising her hand she motioned to him to enter the room. "Come in and sit. Anna will be serving our Sunday dinner momentarily."

Nodding to Aunt Margaret, Cole entered the dining room. "Thank you for inviting me, ma'am."

"You're welcome. I'm sure that the sheriff told you the rule about not leaving a prisoner in jail on a Sunday."

"Yes, she did." Cole grinned. "I'm mighty glad

to be incarcerated here in Surprise. I have to say it's the first time I've ever been let out of jail for a decent meal and to be a guest at such a fine home."

"I'm glad you're so receptive to the idea, Mr. Stanton."

Abigail's anger simmered. How could they converse as if it were the most natural thing to be doing? She was quite certain that criminals were not let out of jail in any other town for Sunday dinners! The muscles in her hand clenched. This was one more thing that she was going to change.

"Abigail, dear?"

"Yes."

"You're hurting my hand."

"Oh my goodness!" Abigail looked down at their hands, she hadn't realized she'd been squeezing so hard. Quickly, releasing it, she patted the paper-thin skin gently, trying to smooth away the red imprint she'd left behind.

"Abigail, sit down."

Taking a seat on her aunt's right, she glanced up to see Cole Stanton looking at her in a way that set her nerves on edge.

He sat across from her, while Mr. Wagner sat at the opposite end of the table. She decided to ignore both of the insufferable men.

"Have you heard from Lydia or Maggie?" she directed to her aunt.

"No, I haven't heard one word from either of

them in weeks. I was hoping they'd be coming along for a visit soon."

Anna, who served as housekeeper, cook and nurse, entered the room pushing a serving cart that carried their steaming dinner. Tall and rail thin, she was attired head to toe in black, looking more like the head of a woman's dormitory rather than someone who was charged with caring for a wealthy sick woman.

"Ah, here's our Anna. The roast smells divine. I wish I had my appetite so that I could enjoy more than just a few morsels." She began to cough softly into a linen handkerchief.

Abigail's heart pulled. Reaching over she touched her aunt's arm. "Anna, please bring aunt some hot lemon tea."

"Add a heaping teaspoon of honey to the cup, Anna," Margaret ordered.

Leaving the serving cart near Mr. Stanton, Anna patted Margaret on the shoulder and left to get the tea.

When the coughing spasm had safely passed, Margaret turned to Mr. Stanton. "Would you be so kind as to carve the roast?"

"He's my prisoner!" The words jumped out of Abigail's mouth. "You can't have him cutting the roast."

"Are you afraid that I might take this carving blade to someone's throat, Sheriff Abigail?"

Chapter Three

Forcing herself to meet his curious gaze, Abigail quickly amended her statement, though it was difficult to keep her voice even. For all they knew Mr. Stanton could be an ax murderer. "What I meant to say was, the carving of the roast should go to someone who is a guest at the table or the man of the household, someone like Mr. Wagner. Perhaps he should cut the roast."

"It's just a piece of meat. I don't see any harm in my cutting the roast!"

"Mr. Stanton, please mind your tone of voice, and Abigail, you would do well to remember your manners." Color rode high on Aunt Margaret's cheeks and Abigail quickly regretted her words. She didn't want to be the cause of another coughing spell.

"I apologize for my rude remarks. Of course Mr. Stanton should carve and serve the roast." Unable to contain herself she added, "Everyone in jail should be given such an honor."

"For goodness sake, Abby. He was charged with drunk and disorderly behavior not murder." Waving her hand towards him, Margaret ordered, "Get on with the task before the food gets cold."

"Yes, ma'am."

He sliced the meat to a perfect thickness and as Margaret passed the plates to him, Cole placed two slices of beef on each one.

"You did a fine job, Mr. Stanton. And might I add, without any extra bloodshed. Good for you."

Beneath his beard Abigail saw him grin. It unnerved her. From across the table his gaze met hers. The grin faded. He placed the carving set back on the cart. She shook out the cloth napkin onto her lap, he did the same. Steaming bowls of potatoes and carrots were passed around the table, the vegetables added to their plates.

Anna brought in the honey-laced lemon tea and wheeled the cart away from the table. There was an awkward moment while grace was said and then the only sound to be heard was the scraping of silverware across the china plates as they started eating.

In between bites, of what was the best meal he'd eaten in a long time, Cole eyed the sheriff. All prim and proper she was, with her hair pulled back in a brown ribbon, the faded brown starched shirt and crisp cotton skirts neat as a pin.

He wondered for the hundredth time how this slip of a woman came to be in such a position?

After swallowing a mouthful of buttermilk biscuit slathered with freshly churned butter, he inquired to no one in particular, "How does a woman come to be a sheriff?"

Abigail's gaze flew from her aunt to Mr. Wagner and back to her aunt again. Cole could just imagine the lump in her throat. It wasn't right for a woman to be involved in the law. Not right at all. As far as he was concerned she had no business being sheriff. From what he'd seen in the few short hours he'd been in this town, Sheriff Abigail was sadly lacking in lawman's skills.

"See, it's like this . . ."

Cole turned his attention to the far end of the table where Mr. Wagner sat balancing a china cup and saucer in his hands. Cole couldn't help noticing that Mr. Wagner seemed to have the answer to everything.

"This is Miss Margaret's town and with her being so sick and all, she had me summon Abigail to come be by her side during her time of need."

Cole couldn't help wondering why Mr. Wagner was being so evasive with his answer?

A coughing spasm shook Miss Margaret's frail

looking form. Abigail left her chair, rushing to her side. "I think you've had enough excitement for one day. Let me get Anna to help put you to bed."

"No. We haven't had dessert yet. Please, let's have our dessert and then I'll go to bed."

Doubt filled Abigail's face, but she finally gave into the older woman, sitting back down in her chair across from Cole. He noticed that she was avoiding his gaze by staring down at her folded hands.

Cole couldn't keep himself from persisting with his questions. He had this burning desire to know how Abigail Monroe came to be in such a position. Didn't they realize the danger in putting such an innocent in that position?

He'd traveled through many a town, large and small. It didn't matter the size or the number of the population, there were always those who just couldn't abide by the law. Abigail Monroe had no idea what she'd gotten herself into.

"Is anyone going to answer my question?" He looked around the table.

"My aunt needed me to help her and I agreed. There's really nothing more to it." She stared across the table at him. "I'll have you know that I am more than qualified for the job."

He studied the matriarch of the household, pointedly ignoring the sheriff. "Miss Margaret? Do you have anything to add?"

"My nieces are devoted to me, Mr. Stanton. Abigail came to me in a time of need. After Sheriff Chauncy died no one wanted to fill the position of lawman. I suppose we really didn't need one, but Abigail was here and there really wasn't enough to keep her occupied in the house."

"Excuse me, ma'am, but this isn't some hobby, like a sewing circle! What if she needs to fire a gun?" He looked at Abigail sitting across from him. He wasn't certain, but he though he detected a steely gleam in those hazel eyes.

"Someone will just have to teach her."

"Who?" he shot back at her.

"I think you could do it, Mr. Stanton. After all you'll need to do something to make up for disturbing the peace."

Abigail sputtered, her face turning a deep shade of red. Her mouth moved, but no words came out. Cole was sure she was going to protest. A woman should know how to shoot if she lived on the open range or in the wilderness, but Surprise appeared to be a civilized town. And Cole couldn't think of a reason for a woman to be carrying a weapon, especially one that was loaded.

"John, see to it that Mr. Stanton teaches the sheriff how to shoot. That will serve nicely as his punishment."

"Now see here!" Cole held his hands up. "I don't want any part of teaching the sheriff about anything."

Margaret began to cough, and this time the coughing didn't seem to want to stop. Anna rushed to her side and wheeled her from the room. At the doorway she angled the chair backwards to ease it from the room and that was when Cole saw it.

Miss Margaret smiled. Oh it was just a little smile, but a smile nonetheless. And if he wasn't mistaken, which he rarely was, there was a definite twinkle in her watery-blue eyes. He stood and rested his elbows on the chair back. Abigail came to stand by him. He could feel her quaking with what he was sure was fury.

Frantically, she began whispering to him, "How could you speak like that? My aunt is a very sick woman! She could be dying!"

Cole stared back at Margaret Sinclair noting how frail she looked with the dark blue comforter pulled up underneath her chin. Her skin looked chalky-white against the deep blue fabric that she held fast in her withered hands. His gaze traveled to her watery-blue eyes and it was there the look of death ended.

Cole had seen death before and he was quite certain that Mrs. Margaret Monroe Sinclair was not dying, least wise not anytime in the near future. The old woman closed her eyelids, shuttering the spark he'd seen moments before, and Anna the dutiful housekeeper took her off to her bedroom.

"I don't think she's going to be dying anytime

soon," he mumbled. Turning around he pasted his most congenial smile on his face, looking at the sheriff of Surprise. "Looks to me like we have an appointment."

"We have no such thing, Mr. Stanton."

Before Cole could respond, Mr. Wagner said, "Now, now, Sheriff Abigail. Don't go getting all upset. Your aunt wants you to have shooting lessons, then so be it. I can't believe that I didn't think of it myself." John pushed away from the table and stood. "We'll do that first thing tomorrow morning."

"Fine." With arms folded across her chest, Abigail glared at Mr. Wagner.

Cole raised his eyebrows in surprise. She gave in so easily. Why, he wondered? Women always seemed to have tricks up their sleeves. He looked at Abigail, as if seeing her for the first time. There didn't seem to be any deep dark secrets or threats or schemes hidden in the depths of her pretty blue-green eyes.

There sure was plenty of anger, though. Now why wasn't she protesting?

"You sure do give in easily."

"I'm not giving in. My aunt has asked that you give me shooting lessons and that is exactly what you'll do. And then you'll be free to go."

"You always do whatever you aunt wants you to do?"

They were walking to the front door, dinner was

clearly over and there wouldn't be any dessert today. Darn he really wanted something sweet. It'd
been a long time since he'd had dessert.

"My aunt is a wonderful, gracious woman. She
means the world to me and I would do anything for
her."

"You'd put yourself in danger for her?"

"There is nothing dangerous about being sheriff
in Surprise. The town is perfectly safe and I'm doing this only until she finds someone who is more
suitable to the position."

Cole grunted. The sheriff was such an innocent,
she didn't even know that her aunt was up to something. He could tell from the glint in Margaret Sinclair's eyes, there was something more going on
here than just a sick old woman wanting her family
gathered around her in a time of need.

It took him a full minute to realize that he'd been
in this town a mere twenty-four hours and already
he was getting involved with things that shouldn't
concern him.

Good thing for him that after tomorrow he'd be
long gone.

Margaret lay in her bed, resting her head against
the three recently plumped feather pillows. All in
all the dinner had gone well, she thought. A slow
smile spread across her withered face. Cole Stanton
was certainly one fine specimen of a man who knew

all the right words to say to bring a blush to a woman's face.

Her smile broadened when she thought how surprised he was going to be in the morning.

A light tapping sounded against the closed bedroom door.

"Enter."

"I'd say that went quite well. Wouldn't you agree?"

Smiling at her dear friend, she motioned for him to sit in the straight backed chair next to her bedside. "It's a start." Fingering the satin edge of the blue comforter, Margaret looked past John, her gaze settling on the view on the other side of the bedroom window.

"I can't let this town die out, John. My nieces are the only hope for Surprise's survival."

Late afternoon sunlight filtered through the swaying leaves of the big old maple tree, casting lacy patterns on the dimpled window panes. Beyond the tree branches she could see the town all laid out like carefully placed pieces of a puzzle. And like a puzzle her plans were slowly coming together.

"Mr. Stanton seems to be on the up and up. With the exception of his excesses of last night," John added, thoughtfully.

"Yes. Did you happen to find out why he was so intoxicated?"

John scratched his chin, thoughtfully. "I think he

was heard ranting about having everything stolen from him."

"I suppose that could be reason enough to over imbibe." She paused, lost in thought and then said, "He'll do quite nicely for our Abigail." Margaret's statement was a simple one. "It's interesting, the way he just happened to land himself here in our little town."

"A providence of fate, it would seem."

Winking at her friend, she said, "Fate, my dear, John, is a wonderful part of life."

"Yes, but what if it doesn't work in our favor?"

"Then we'll just have to help it along."

"You mean by making him give her shooting lessons?"

Turning her gaze to meet his, Margaret replied, "Exactly. I didn't see any need for him to know that our Abigail just happens to be a crack shot."

Their laughter rang throughout the bedroom. Rubbing his hands together, John added, "I can't wait to see his reaction when he learns that Abigail can outshoot most men."

"What if she tells him ahead of time?"

"She won't."

"How can you be so certain?"

"Because, John, Abigail will want to show him up. She's still so mad at her ex-fiance Edwin, she's not about to let any man take advantage of her any time soon."

"Tomorrow will be soon enough to see what happens."

"Yes, we will wait for tomorrow," Margaret agreed.

Chapter Four

It was cold. A bitter wind cut across the yard causing Cole to fight his way back to the front door. His
family needed him to bring more firewood. He was
all they had left. It was up to him to keep them warm
and safe, to bring them back to life. He saw his
sister Annie first. Her tiny body sprawled across
their mother's lap—a lifeless bundle wrapped in a
threadbare blanket.

Then he saw where his mother's hand lay still in
death, stopping in mid-stroke. The racking spasms
of father's coughing reached his ear. He wanted to
run from the sound, he wanted to leave this for
someone else to take care of. Outside the wind
howled, a tree limb banged against the rough wood
siding. Behind him the door flew open, as a fierce

gust of wind rushed into the room lifting the blanket off his sister's tiny form.

And then he saw for the first time all that remained of her was a pile of bones. Despite the cold, beads of sweat broke out on his brow. Cole tried to move, but his feet were frozen to the planked floorboards.

Then he heard his own voice break through the bleakness that had become death. "I brought the wood, just like you wanted, Papa. See, I brought the wood." The heavy logs rolled out of his arms onto the floor. Everything had turned to ice. A thin coating covered his father's body, and then encased his mother and sister.

Cole opened his mouth to scream, but the words were frozen in his throat. His chest tightened as if someone had a vise around him. He couldn't breath. He wanted to die. A low moaning sound broke through the silence. Tears began streaming down his face.

Feeling a hand on his shoulder, Cole turned, hoping the person had come to bring life back to his family.

"Wake up. Mr. Stanton, wake up."

He wanted to leave this nightmare. To leave behind the despair and gut wrenching pain that he felt every time he entered here, but it was so hard to let go. This was the only chance he had to see his family again. Even seeing them as they were in death was better than nothing at all.

"No!"

"Mr. Stanton, please."

Struggling from the grips of sleep, Cole fought against the hand the held his shoulder. "Don't leave me . . ."

"Cole, wake up. It's just a bad dream. Wake up."

The shaking continued. Turning on his side toward the sound of the voice, he heard the silken tones calling him—the voice like a soothing balm on an open wound. Slowly, opening his eyes he looked out through the blurry haze of sleep.

A young woman was kneeling by his bedside. The sunlight streaming through the window behind her cast golden highlights through her dark hair. Staring into those hazel eyes, he saw compassion and concern. Her one hand was still resting lightly on his shoulder, while the other reached out to touch his face.

In the full minute it took him to remember where he was, Cole put a tight clamp on his emotions. "Don't." Batting her hand away from his face, Cole rolled onto his back. He didn't want or need her touch.

"I'm sorry. You were having a bad dream. I heard you yelling even before I came in to the jail."

"Look, Sheriff. I don't need you worrying about me."

Her shadow fell across him as she stood. "Fine. As soon as you're ready you can give me my shooting lesson. Then you're free to leave Surprise."

He could tell by the catch in her voice she was upset. Cole hardened his heart, telling himself it didn't matter that he'd hurt her feelings. She'd no business caring about him one way or the other. He was just another drifter passing through town.

He would teach her how to shoot, fulfilling the agreement he'd made yesterday at Miss Margaret's house. Then he would leave this strange little town, move on, find another place to settle down and start over again. Rising from the bed, Cole found himself standing toe-to-toe with Sheriff Abigail.

She was wearing yet another hideous dress. This one was gray in color and looked as if it had seen one too many creek-side washings. He couldn't help wondering if she thought this was how a lady sheriff was supposed to look. At least, today, she wore her hair down so that it fell softly around her shoulders.

The sound of her voice quickly reminded him that he was staring at her.

"Is something wrong, Mr. Stanton?"

"I just need to visit the outhouse."

Quickly she stepped aside, letting him pass through the open cell door. "Don't go wandering off," she warned him needlessly.

Where would he go?

"Aunt Margaret sent some rolls and jam for your breakfast."

He looked over his shoulder at her. "Bless her heart for thinking of me." What was it with that old woman? He wanted to ask her if Miss Margaret treated all the criminals with such generosity, but he just shook his head deciding it wasn't worth the effort and went outside.

By the time he came back his breakfast was all laid out for him, and right next to the smallest Derringer he'd ever seen. With his hands on his hips, Cole looked to the other side of the desk where Sheriff Abigail was standing looking mighty pleased.

It was the first time he'd seen her smile. Taking in the sight of her upturned mouth and the twin dimples that appeared on either side set Cole to thinking about his other appetite. It'd been a while since he'd kissed a woman. He'd lay odds that Abigail's mouth tasted just as sweet as strawberry jam.

Hoping to distract himself from those thoughts, he picked up a roll, and grabbed hold of the flat knife lying by the side of the plate, plunging it into a little bowl of strawberry jam.

Slathering the berry-filled jam on the roll, he thought about how good her smile looked. It was too bad that he was going to be the one to make it go away.

Speaking through a mouthful of sweet jam and a generous bite of his roll, he said, "You can't use that gun."

Folding her arms across her chest, she said, "Yes, I can."

Swallowing, he leveled a dark gaze on her. "No, you can't."

"I don't see why not. It's a perfectly fine weapon. Even Mr. Jules, at the mercantile, said the weapon was suited for me."

Finishing off the roll, Cole continued to stare at her, noticing the way she was smirking at him. Reaching out his arm, he snatched the pitiful Derringer from the desk top. "It's too small. Come on. We're returning this."

With two long strides he was at the door. "Are you coming or not?" He turned to find her still standing behind the desk. Little splotches of red marked her face. Uh oh, she was getting all worked up.

"Mr. Stanton, you are not the one giving orders around here, I am. You would do well to remember that. You don't think I'd let you go off on your own now do you?"

"Right, and no I don't think you'd let me go off by myself. I might try to escape."

She ignored his last comment. "You can go over to the mercantile with me and help me select a more appropriate gun."

Cole held the door open as Abigail stalked by with her head held high and her spine ramrod straight. Cole smiled. She sure did have her pride, he'd give her that. They crossed the street and entered Mr. Jules' mercantile. Cole waited until they were at the counter and then handed the sheriff her weapon.

"Thank you." She took the gun from him, looking at him with those hazel eyes. He couldn't tell what she was thinking.

"It's going to be *your* gun. You tell him it's not the right one for you."

Sheriff Abigail held the gun in the flattened palm of her hand. Cole waited for her to say something, but the minutes ticked by as she appeared to be pondering the situation.

The black curtains that separated the storeroom from the store parted and Mr. Jules stepped behind the counter. "Good morning, Sheriff." He nodded in Cole's general direction.

"Good morning, Mr. Jules."

"What brings you here on this fine morning?" Noticing the gun in her hand, he asked, "Is there a problem with the Derringer?"

"It's too small." She winked slyly at Mr. Jules.

The man looked mystified. He studied Abigail's outstretched hand and then glanced nervously in Cole's direction looking for help. "Hmm . . . I see."

"It's quite simple, Mr. Jules. According to Mr. Stanton, this gun doesn't suit me."

Cole was standing a foot away from Abigail, his back turned to the counter so he could look down the aisles at the merchandise and still coach the sheriff. Casting a glance over his shoulder, he looked at Mr. Jules.

He kept glancing at Cole and then back to Abigail. Cole just shrugged like he'd no idea what this woman was thinking. Beneath the growth of beard his mouth curved into a smile.

"Mr. Jules, I need . . . ," her voice trailed off as she cast a sideways glance at Cole.

"A Colt .45." Cole's mouth barely moved as he told her what to say.

"Oh yes, that's right, I need a Colt .45. Silly me, I always have such trouble remembering which gun is which." The Derringer was slapped on the counter for emphasis.

Cole could have sworn he'd detected a note of sarcasm in her tone. Wary, he continued to advise her on the sly. "Tell him you need a shotgun. Something small but built for the job."

"I guess if Mr. Stanton is right, I'll need a shotgun. Please, make sure it's small, but well built . . . for *my* job."

He quirked one eyebrow, amused. She was really taking to this.

Mr. Jules was looking at her as if she'd gone plum loco.

Cole watched in amazement as the sheriff began to shake. Was she laughing? Then she took a deep breath as if to steady herself. Placing her hands flat on the surface of the scarred countertop, she leaned over it, leveling her gaze on Mr. Jules.

"I am the Sheriff of this town. I'm here to serve and protect the citizens. Now I ask you, how am I supposed to do that with a weapon that's too small?" She didn't wait for him to answer. "Give me a Colt .45, a Winchester shotgun, and a supply of ammunition for both."

Seeing that she was on a roll, Cole added, "And a penny's worth of that red licorice." He pointed to a jar resting on the middle shelf behind the counter.

Without batting an eye, she ordered, "Put it on Miss Margaret's account."

"No need. The town is supposed to supply the weapons for the sheriff." Mr. Jules moved swiftly through the curtained-off area, returning with Abigail's order.

They were about to leave, when Abigail said, "The red licorice, please."

Grabbing a small brown paper bag, Mr. Jules filled it with the candy. Abigail took it from his outstretched hand and gave it to Cole.

He smiled down at her and then peered into the

sack. It was filled with far more than a penny's worth of candy. "I'd say it pays to be around the Sheriff of Surprise."

"Don't look so smug, Mr. Stanton. You still have to give me my shooting lessons. Consider the candy part of your payment."

"There is the small matter of my freedom."

"Yes, there is that to consider," she sniffed.

Cole followed her around to the back of the store. She stalked towards a split rail fence that separated the dirt yard from a large field of clover. Leaning the Winchester against the rail, she gingerly slid the handgun out of her skirt pocket.

Seeing her take the weapon out reminded him that she'd need a holster.

As she held the gun in her hand, Abigail had to bite her upper lip to keep from smiling. Cole Stanton had no idea that she was about to put one over on him. Letting him think that she'd no idea how to shoot was more fun than she deserved to be having on such a fine spring morning. She'd liked the little gun. It had fit perfectly into the palm of her hand. Of course the larger .45 Colt was more suited to her job and would be her gun of choice from now on.

Testing the weight of the gun in her hand, she turned around on her heel, regarding Mr. Stanton through half-drawn eyelids. Intent on studying the

Winchester, he didn't notice her perusal of him. His boots were worn so there was barely any thickness left to the soles. The denim Levis that he wore fit him loosely, like he'd recently lost some weight. They were worn and patched so many times that Abigail couldn't tell where the original fabric began.

His blue chambray shirt was tucked into the waistband of the pants. A soft spring breeze blew by. It ruffled the cotton fabric, flirting with the material, flattening it over his broad chest and muscular shoulders. Abigail swallowed.

Tufts of dark curly hair stuck out from the collar of Mr. Stanton's shirt. Her gaze followed the trail leading to the thick dark beard that covered most of his face. She wondered what he looked like beneath all that hair. At first glance, she thought his nose was straight, but then she saw the bump near the top. She wondered how he'd broken it? In a bar brawl no doubt.

Her next breath froze in her chest as she found herself looking into those dark eyes. One of his eyebrows shot up as he stared back at her. The heat of a blush spread over her face. She'd been caught.

"Is there a problem, Sheriff?" he drawled.

Shaking her head, she turned away, mortified that she'd been caught staring. There was something about the man that set her heart to racing just a little faster than normal. Surprised by the realization, she cleared her thoughts by looking along the ground for some tin cans. Scrounging up four of them, Abigail carefully balanced each on the top rail of the fence.

"We can start with the shotgun." Cole walked up behind her.

She turned to face him. He was right in front of her a mere arm's reach away. She imagined that she could feel the heat from his body. Leveling her gaze on him, she said, "No. We'll start with the Colt."

"All right, I can do that."

She watched him place the shotgun alongside of the fence, and took the Colt out of her pocket. The familiar weight of the gun in her hand made Abigail feel powerful. She liked knowing that with one twitch of her finger she could drop a man like a dead fly. This was what she'd needed two nights ago when she'd arrested Mr. Stanton. With this weapon by her side there wouldn't be one person who didn't take her seriously.

Abigail would never be laughed at again, least wise not while doing her job. So engrossed was she, that Abigail hadn't realize Mr. Stanton was talking to her until she heard him call her name.

"Sheriff! You're not listening to a word I've been saying."

With his hands planted firmly on his hips and his legs spread apart, Cole glared at her. "This is important. I don't want you shooting anybody's head off. That includes mine! So listen up, lady!"

"There's no need to speak to me in that tone of voice, Mr. Stanton." The man was infuriating. Abigail wondered how it was that a few minutes ago she'd felt some sort of an attraction to him. Now she just wanted these *lessons* to be over with.

"Look, shooting can be dangerous business."

As if she didn't already know that. Abigail was dying to show him a thing or two about shooting. Her Uncle Chester Sinclair had taught her at an early age how to handle a variety of weapons. There were many summers where she'd left more than one mark in the trees out in the backyard of Aunt Margaret's house.

Mr. Stanton came towards her holding a small box of bullets. "I'm going to tell you how to load your weapon." Nodding at the gun, he opened the box and counted six bullets into his hand.

"Take these, roll the chamber open and place one in each hole."

A shudder of excitement raced along her spine, she found herself enjoying the deception. Reaching out she took the bullets and did as he instructed, feigning interest. He then explained in great detail the workings of the gun and before she knew what was happening he'd turned her around so she was facing the tin cans.

"I think you're standing too close to me, Mr. Stanton." She imagined she could feel the brush of denim and heat of his legs against the back of hers.

"Sorry about that, Sheriff."

Sucking in a deep breath, Abigail waited for him to move away. He seemed to settle in even closer to her. His chest was pressed against her back and he brought his arms around either side of her. Taking both of her hands in his, he raised their arms until the gun was level with her shoulders.

Oh, dear, perhaps she'd let this little charade go too far.

Chapter Five

The sun had risen to above the tree line. But Abigail was sure the heat she was feeling wasn't coming from the sun's rays. Hard muscled arms were encircling her body and she was too afraid to move away from them.

"Now, look through the sight, just like I explained." The sound of his voice, so close to her ear, sent goosebumps rolling along the skin on her arms.

The index finger on his right hand moved to cover hers and before she knew what was happening the trigger twitched and the gun went off. The action sent her back against the hard wall of his chest. Abigail gasped in surprise, unprepared for the kick. It was all Mr. Stanton's fault for distracting her.

"Did I hit anything?" she asked, hoping for the best, knowing that her aim had been way off.

"No. The shot went wide."

"Maybe, it would be better if I tried it by myself."

Stepping away from her, he said, "Suit yourself."

With the butt of the gun balanced in her hand, Abigail practiced taking aim at the tin can closet to her. Smiling from the sheer delight of just holding this weapon, she squinted down the short barrel of the Colt. With the can firmly in her sights, she squeezed the trigger. The gun went off leaving a puff of smoke in its wake. This time she was ready for the kick and managed to stay standing with her legs braced slightly apart.

Frowning, she looked at the small branch of the oak tree as it fluttered to the ground, muttering, "I'm out of practice." Speaking for his benefit, she said, "Darn! I thought my aim was better."

"You pulled your arms up when the trigger went off. Concentrate on holding steady."

Cocking the gun, she only pretended to be listening to his advice, determined this time to knock the can clean off the rail. Repeating the process, Abigail smiled in satisfaction when the bullet hit its mark, knocking the first tin can clean off the fence.

She let out a "Whoop!" and spun around to look at Mr. Stanton.

"Lucky shot." He grinned at her. "Try it again. But watch where you point that thing!"

Lucky shot, indeed! Thanks to Uncle Chester's persistence, all those hours of practice paid off. However, anxious to show up Mr. Stanton, she let him have it with both barrels, so to speak, knocking off not only the next can in line, but the last two hit the ground with a satisfying thud too.

"Well, I'll be . . ." he rubbed a hand along his bearded chin. Maybe it was only chance that she'd hit all three cans, but Cole wanted to be sure.

With only two bullets remaining in the chamber, he told her to reload and went to set up some more cans. Standing by her side once again, he looked down to check her stance. It was when he was checking her form and hand position on the gun that he caught it.

Looking into those blue-green eyes, it struck him; Abigail Monroe was seeing only the targets. In her eyes he saw determination the likes of which he'd never seen before. So focused was she on those cans, that she didn't notice the small crowd that had begun gathering at the edge of the lot.

He hoped that she was as good a shot with an audience as she had been a few minutes before when it was just him looking on. "Go ahead, Sheriff, knock 'em down."

Stepping aside, Cole folded his arms across his chest and waited. Her first big test of courage and strength as a lawman or rather law-woman was here and Cole doubted that the lady was even aware of the moment. If she managed to hit all or even most of those cans, her reputation as peacemaker would be set, least wise in Surprise. On the other hand if she missed all those targets, she'd end up being ostracized and would earn little respect from the townsfolk.

He didn't realize until she started firing that he was praying for the former to happen. Amidst the dust and the sounds of metal hitting tin, it was hard to tell what was happening. As the dust settled and the crowd held its collective breath, Cole took a step towards the sheriff.

"Wow." His breath whooshed out of him when he saw all but three of the cans lying on the ground. Two of the three left standing had been nicked. Without thinking he strode to the sheriff and picked her up, swung her around, all the while whooping and yelling!

"You did it, honey girl!"

Behind them the crowd cheered. Abigail's eyes widened when she realized she'd had an audience. "Put me down, Mr. Stanton, please."

Cole set her on her feet, but didn't let her go. Reaching out his hand, he touched the side of her face, and after tucking an errant strand of hair behind her ear, he smiled at her. "Well done, Sheriff."

Her face was flushed and he could well imagine that her pulse was racing with excitement. Abigail stood there looking up at him, and reflected in the sheriff's eyes he saw her pride and suddenly realized that he shared the feeling.

Reining in his emotions, he stepped aside, letting the townsfolk congratulate their sheriff. Abigail was shaking hands with Mr. Jules when Cole turned away from the scene. He'd done his job and served his time, now it was time for him to move on.

His escape was intercepted by John Wagner.

"I say, Mr. Stanton, are you leaving Surprise so soon."

"Mr. Wagner, my time here is done. I've gotten myself drunk and arrested. Had a nice Sunday dinner at Miss Margaret's and taught your sheriff to shoot a weapon." Looking back over his shoulder at Abigail, he added as an afterthought, "Though she didn't need much coaching from me. It's more than time that I move along."

Leaning in close to him John, said, "She didn't need any coaching from you."

"What's that supposed to mean?" It may have been long in coming but the realization hit him like a brick; he'd been duped. Rather than being angry, though, he found himself smiling.

"So, I take it this means that your Sheriff Abigail was already a crack shot?"

Grinning, John nodded. "Yup, has been since she was about ten years old."

Glancing to where she stood with the townspeople, Cole mumbled, "Well, I'll be . . ."

And that cinched it for him. Cole couldn't stay a minute longer in this town. For the first time in a very long while he was starting to care about people. The painful memory of losing his family loomed and Cole felt as if he didn't have the strength to open his life or heart to anyone again. Thoughts of regret about leaving Surprise didn't even half begin to cover what he was feeling.

He'd love to have seen what Sheriff Abigail was truly made of and maybe he would have taken more than a little delight at pestering her some more.

It *was* time to go. He didn't want or need any emotional attachments.

Abigail leaned against the side of the building, watching as Cole Stanton waited on the platform of the train depot. The weight of the .45 and brand new leather holster hung snugly about her hips. She'd found the holster on her desk when she'd gone back to the sheriff's office. There'd been no name or note attached to the gesture, though she suspected it was Cole Stanton who'd left it.

Off in the distance, the shrill sound of the whistle of the noon Lowland Express bounced off the craggy hillside of the Catskill Mountains, echoing along the valley.

Soon, he would leave.

Instead of feeling the relief that she'd expected at his departure, Abigail was surprised to find herself a little disappointed. She should be thinking, good riddance. Bolstering herself against the side of the building, Abigail waited for the train to arrive, her thoughts wandering over the events of the morning.

All in all, it had been a great morning. Silently she thanked her uncle for all those shooting lessons. Of course she'd no way of knowing, until today, that she'd had it in her to shoot like a man. A smug smile of satisfaction settled around her mouth—she was a better shot than most men she knew.

That may not be saying much, considering she only knew a few men including John Wagner and Edwin, but she'd stunned Cole Stanton with her sure shots and that was something.

All morning she'd tried to forget how his arms had felt around her. The memory of the way his hand had covered hers, when he was showing her how to hold the gun, was enough to send shivers along her spine. Edwin Quinn had never made her feel that way.

The only thing he'd made her feel was inadequate. If he could see her now, Abigail wondered what he would think. She had to be crazy standing here worrying over what Edwin thought of her. The man had broken her heart.

As for Cole Stanton, she shouldn't be feeling

anything for him. Not one person in this town knew anything at all about the drifter. He could be a murdering thief. The thought was enough to remind her that it was time for the man to be moving on.

The train whistle sounded again. Abigail looked up to see the puff of steam coming from the engine as the train made its way into Surprise. Amidst the hissing of steam and the screeching of the brakes, the train engine ground to a stop in front of the outhouse-sized station.

Passengers began to disembark from the train. Quickly, she scanned the platform searching for Mr. Stanton. He was nowhere in sight, so Abigail assumed that he was safely on board the train.

Relieved that he was finally gone, she turned and went back to the Sheriff's office. An updated delivery of Wanted posters had arrived and she wanted to take a look at them. Through the rays of the shifting morning sunlight, dust motes floated down onto the desk top, landing on the stack of papers that Abigail had been studying. Taking a much needed break, she rubbed her eyelids with her fingertips. Then looking down, she flipped the next sheaf of paper over, and her heart jumped to her throat.

Chapter Six

Cole knew that the Sheriff was watching him. His mouth twitched beneath his beard. She sure as heck had him fooled into thinking that she knew nothing about guns. The sheriff had more gumption than he'd thought possible.

The Lowland Express pulled to a stop amidst a cloud of rolling steam from the engine and the sound of squealing brakes. He had to wait for several minutes while the passengers disembarked, surprised at the number of people getting off the train. For a small, secluded town, Surprise sure did get its share of visitors.

"Why if it isn't Cole Stanton, as I live and breathe!"

He spun around to find the source of the feminine

voice and found himself almost on top of a voluptuous red-headed woman. "Miss McCurdy. It is still Miss, isn't it?" Cole tipped his head to one side, studying the familiar face before him.

"Of course I'm still single, Cole. You know I'm saving myself for you." Playfully, she slapped his arm with her white gloved hand. Brushing her ample bosom against his chest, she added, "I'm so happy to have stumbled upon you. I was afraid that this would turn out to be just another dead-end town. But if you're here, I daresay, there must be something exciting happening!"

Cole looked at her, noticing the fine wrinkles around her brown eyes. The heavy coal that she'd used to outline her eyes only accentuated the lines. Her cheeks were dotted with red rouge; her full lips were painted yet another shade of red.

"How'd you find this place, Wanda?" Cole asked, dropping the pretense of formality.

Batting her lashes at him, she moistened her lips with a slow seductive sweep of her tongue. "I didn't follow you, if that's what you're thinking. I came because of an advertisement in this newspaper."

Reaching into one of her traveling bags, Wanda pulled out a sheaf of yellowed newspaper. "See right here on page three." She stabbed at the paper with her finger.

Cole took the paper out of her hand and skimmed

the advertisement. Sure enough there was mention of the town of Surprise. Words like *burgeoning* and *exciting* were used to describe the place. Along with phrases like; *make your dreams come true* and *settle in a place where crime is non-existent.*

Anger pulled at him. Whoever had dreamed up this advertisement was all but inviting criminals to put down roots in this town. The sheriff, even if she was a sure shot, would be no match for the hooligans that were sure to flock here once word got out. He shoved the paper back at Wanda, eyeing her coolly.

"So you're thinking about settling here?"

"Now, that all depends, on whether or not you'll be sticking around." She batted her lashes at him.

He wouldn't be staying here. He would continue on to the next town. Maybe set up another contracting business. Building, working with his hands, an honest day's work—one that left him feeling satisfied. That's what he needed to do.

After all, the sheriff had made herself pretty clear on her wishes to see him ride out of town on a rail, literally. While the train sat idling on the track he looked around the platform. There were still a few stragglers getting off the train, so he had a few more minutes to decide what he was going to do.

A slip of a redhead was making her way down the steps of the last car. Wanda followed his gaze.

"She doesn't look to be your type, honey. Why don't you reconsider and stay a bit longer? We sure could teach these townsfolk a thing or two."

He knew she was referring to the time they'd spent together in Albany, going from saloon to saloon, carousing the night away. He was through with that kind of life.

"I don't think so, Wanda." With a tip of his hat, he headed to the last compartment. The young woman stumbled over one of the two valises that she was trying to carry off the train.

"Let me give you a hand." Reaching up, Cole took the bag out of her hand. She was a pretty little thing. But it was the set of her eyes that made him wonder, who did she remind him of?

"It's very kind of you, sir. I have to say this trip never gets any easier. I don't know what to expect with this mountain weather so I usually pack everything I own."

Cole frowned at her as she chattered on.

Seeing the look of doubt on his face, she added, "Well, perhaps not *everything*. Oh, you do know what I mean." With a swish of her green skirts she was safely off the train.

Turning she took the bag from his hand. "My, you are a handsome one. Are you sure you have to leave Surprise?"

Cole grinned at her harmless flirtations. "I have to go."

"Thank you for your help, Mister . . . ? You do have a name don't you?"

"Stanton. Cole Stanton."

"Thank you Mr. Stanton for assisting me. It was very gentlemanly of you. Have a safe trip." She flashed him a brilliant smile.

He stood there for a few more minutes and watched her sashay away. Shaking his head at her friendly outgoing manner, he turned and went to find a seat thinking that Sheriff Abigail could take a few lessons from that young woman. Sighing, he leaned his head against the seat back.

It wasn't long before doubts began swirling around in his mind. What was Abigail going to do with this sudden influx of people?

Would she really be able to protect herself and the town?

Stretching out his long legs, he crossed one foot over the other. It wasn't his problem. The seat shuddered as the train pulled away from the station. Tension stretched between his shoulder blades.

He should be feeling relief. Here he was embarking on another journey, his life was before him. But it was what Cole was leaving behind him that was bothering the heck out of him.

Abigail read the Wanted poster through a third time, hardly able to believe that she'd let this criminal slip away. Oh my, what had she done? She'd actually been at the train station and allowed him to board the train. Grabbing her hat off the desk, slapping it on her head, she raced out the door and almost tripped over her cousin.

"Lydia!"

"Abigail. Look at you the town's sheriff! I could hardly believe you'd done this when I'd read the letter Aunt Margaret sent. I had to come and see for myself."

Giving her a quick hug, Abigail hurried to explain her hasty departure. "I can't talk to you right now, Lydia. I have a criminal and a train to catch."

By the time she reached the platform the train had long left the station and was disappearing over Dawson's Ridge. Turning, she ran over to the mercantile.

Pushing through the doorway, she stopped to catch her breath. Sucking air into her lungs, she shouted, "Mr. Jules! Mr. Jules! I need you to come with me this instant."

"What's wrong?"

Running down the dry goods aisle, she went around the back of the counter and grabbed the man by the arm. "I'll explain to you on the way to catch the train."

"What train?"

"Come along, Mr. Jules. We can't waste any more time."

By the time they'd managed to get the wagon

hitched to a team of horses and started to move out of town, Abigail could see only a small puff of steam trailing the train, which was growing smaller and smaller as it chugged on to it's next stop.

"Hurry up! He's going to get away."

"Who is going to get away?"

"Cole Stanton."

Mr. Jules slapped the reins against the backside of the horse. "Yah! Yah!" he yelled. The horses picked up their pace, but Abigail was afraid they'd be too late to apprehend Mr. Stanton.

She grabbed the side of the wagon seat as they gained momentum.

"There's a steep grade coming up. We'll be able to catch up to them there," Mr. Jules assured her.

Sure enough, a few minutes later the train came into view. As they drew closer, Abigail tried to plan out what she was going to say to Mr. Stanton.

After running a few ideas through her mind, she decided that the direct approach would be best. "Pull up alongside the train, Mr. Jules."

With the reins gripped between his fingers, he jerked his head around to look at her. "Are you crazy? I can't pull up alongside a moving train."

Ignoring his concern, she shouted above the noise of the train, "Just pull up next to the train!"

As the engine began its ascent the speed began to slacken, giving her the opportunity to try to stand up. She managed to get far enough up to see into the windows of the cars. She began searching for Mr. Stanton. When she didn't see him in the last car, she urged Mr. Jules on.

"Sit down, Sheriff."

Ignoring his order, she continued to look into the windows of the next car. Her gaze settled on a lone man, sitting in the middle of the car. He appeared to be sleeping with his hat pulled low over his brow; she'd recognize his form anywhere. Cole Stanton. She had him right where she wanted him. Well, almost. Where she really wanted him was back in jail where he belonged.

As the train slowed, Mr. Jules was able to bring the wagon right up to a set of steps. "I'm getting off. You go on ahead and tell the engineer to stop."

"What do you mean you're getting off?"

Abigail didn't have time to argue with him.

Repositioning herself in the wagon, she waited until they were right by the steps and then carefully stepped onto the moving train. Waving Mr. Jules on, with her gun drawn, she found her way into the car where Mr. Stanton was sleeping.

Using the toe of her boot, she gave him a swift kick in the shin. Pushing the brim of his hat back, he opened his eyes, staring down the barrel of a gun. Slowly, deliberately, he let his gaze wander up the gun, over her hand, until finally he was looking her right in the eye.

Pushing himself up to sit straighter in the seat, he said, "Good afternoon, Sheriff."

"Good afternoon, Mr. Stanton."

Looking into those dark eyes, she imagined him thinking that he could charm his way out of this latest dilemma.

A slow seductive smile crept across his face. "Did you miss me already?"

Annoyed when he really did put on a charming front, she replied, "No. I'm placing you under arrest."

Normally she would have expected a person might be upset by the fact that their newly won freedom was about to be taken away. But then she was dealing with Cole Stanton and knew from experience there wasn't much he found unsettling.

Folding his arms across his chest, he appeared to be nonchalant about the issue. "What for?"

"Cole Stanton, you are under arrest for robbery. Please stand up, sir."

"Robbery! I haven't committed any such crime."

"I'm afraid that according to this," she drew a folded piece of paper out of her pocket, taking great satisfaction in snapping it open in front of his face, "you fit the description of a man who robbed a jewelry store in Albany last month."

Snatching the poster from her outstretched hand, he skimmed the page. "This could be anybody."

"No, Mr. Stanton, I'm afraid that this would be you."

Taking the poster back, she tucked it back in her pocket. Then lowering the gun, aiming in the general vicinity of his heart, she ordered, "Please, stand up, Mr. Stanton. You are under arrest for the robbery of the Fisk Jewelry store of State Street in Albany, New York."

Chapter Seven

It had been a week since Cole's arrest and it seemed most of the townsfolk had been in to visit. Some were openly curious about who he was, while others were actually laying odds as to how long he would remain in jail this time. John Wagner had stopped by twice to play chess with him through the bars. Cole had won both times.

Cole had found out that the pretty redhead he'd met coming off the train last week was Lydia Louise Monroe, one of Abigail's two cousins. She'd walked past the office a couple of times, but had yet to come in to formally introduce herself.

And then there was Wanda McCurdy. She'd been by to visit him three times since his unfortunate incarceration. The more he spoke to her the more he was beginning to think that Miss McCurdy was up to something. He'd met more than a few scam artists in his travels and while Wanda didn't exactly fit the bill, Cole suspected she knew how to run a successful game.

One thing was for certain, Cole was tired of being locked up. He was hoping he'd be able to convince the sheriff that he wasn't the one who'd robbed the jewelry store. However, Sheriff Abigail was hardly speaking to him, so that left him with little opportunity to state his case.

Rising from the cot he extended his arms above his head and stretched, groaning a bit as his joints popped in relief. He wondered why the sheriff wasn't in the office yet? You could set your watch by her arrival and departure. In the office by nine o'clock in the morning, out the door at three in the afternoon, probably for tea with her aunt and cousin, and then she was back for one last check before leaving for the day at seven in the evening.

He looked up at the clock on the wall. It was 9:30 and still no sign of the woman. Frowning, he wondered why he even cared. It was her fault he was here in the first place. He shouldn't give two cents worth of his time worrying over her absence.

Just as these thoughts were crossing his mind, the door opened and in walked the woman of his recent meanderings.

"Morning, Sheriff."

"Good Morning, Mr. Stanton."

Right away he noticed that there was something different about her. It wasn't her dress that was for sure. She still wore the same drab attire she'd had on the first time they'd met. Leaning against the cool steel bars, he stuck his arms between them, resting his elbows on a cross bar.

"Is there a problem, Mr. Stanton?" Her voice was soft, but there was no mistaking the steely tone.

She was wearing her hair in a different fashion. He was surprised that he hadn't noticed it right away. "No. No problem. I was just admiring your hair." She'd braided it in one long single braid that fell down her back skimming her waistline. There was a pretty plum-colored piece of satin tied off in a neat bow at the bottom.

Her cheeks colored in a soft rose shade. He enjoyed the fact that his comment made her blush.

Turning, she met his gaze. "You shouldn't be looking at my hair."

"I don't see why not. There isn't a whole lot for me to look at in here that I haven't already seen before." He grinned beneath his thick beard. He so enjoyed bantering with her.

Her expression was contrite when she replied, "I apologize for your state of boredom. Perhaps the circuit judge will be here soon."

"Do you have any idea when that might be?"

"I'm afraid not. I've no way of knowing the judge's schedule."

"You do have a telegraph office in Surprise. Why don't you just send him a message?"

Patiently, like he were a schoolboy, she explained, "By the time a message reached him he would more than likely be moving along to his next stop. And by the time it was relayed along, he'd probably be riding into our town anyway. So you see there's no point in going to all the trouble."

He would have liked nothing more than to while away his morning getting into a lengthy debate with her, but just then the door burst open.

"Abigail, I've come for a visit." On those words, Lydia Monroe sailed into the room like she was going to visit the Queen of England.

Her thick red hair was piled on top of her head in a bundle of curls. She wore a crisp yellow skirt and matching jacket. Cole stared from her to Abigail unable to believe that the two women shared the same blood.

She flashed him a brilliant smile, fastening her green eyes on him with such intensity that a lesser man may have blushed.

"I don't believe I've been formally introduced to your guest, Abigail."

"Goodness, you sound just like Aunt Margaret.

Cole, I mean Mr. Stanton, is not a guest in this town, he is a prisoner!"

"And I should say he's a mighty handsome one!"

"Lydia!"

Sashaying over to him, she stuck her gloved hand through the bars. "I apologize for not introducing myself the other day at the station. I'm Abigail's cousin, Lydia Louise Monroe."

Taking her hand in his, he said, "Nice to meet you again."

"Same here, Mr. Stanton." Leaning in close to him, she whispered, "Isn't our Abigail just the prettiest sheriff you've ever seen?"

Releasing her hand he answered, "Prettiest sheriff I've met."

"If it would help you, I could vouch for your character. Then maybe Abigail would let you out for good behavior."

He remembered the first encounter they'd had. It was the day he was leaving town and she'd nearly fallen off the train. He'd helped her with her baggage.

"I appreciate your offer, Miss Monroe. But I seriously doubt the Sheriff will care. She's very by the book if you know what I mean."

"Indeed, I do." Lydia turned away from him and walked over to Abigail's desk. "Did you have a chance to speak to Aunt Margaret this morning?"

Abigail looked from Cole to Lydia and back again. She didn't like having them so friendly with one another. "No."

The truth was she'd been avoiding both her aunt and Lydia for the past two days. She'd been keeping a close eye on some of the newcomers, Mr. Stanton's friend Wanda McCurdy being one of them. In addition to this she had also been devising a way to get her prisoner out of jail for a few hours a day.

"Oh." Lydia seemed to be disappointed by her response.

Nibbling on her lower lip, Lydia ran her finger along the corner of the desk. *Oh dear.* Abigail knew all the signs and they were there. Lydia always nibbled her lip when she was trying not to tell a secret.

"Is there something I should know about?" Abigail began to worry. Perhaps Aunt Margaret's health had taken a turn.

Before Lydia could answer, John Wagner entered the office. "Morning, Sheriff, Miss Lydia, Mr. Stanton."

"Good morning, Mr. Wagner. I'm glad you're here, I have something to tell you." Abigail had been working for several days on her new idea and now was as good a time as any to announce her plan.

Taking his hat off, John set it on the desk and

ran a hand through his rumpled hair. He looked more than a little curious.

"Out with it!"

"Won't you sit down?" Extending her hand, she offered him her seat, enjoying having control over the situation. It was the first time in a long time where she could remember Mr. Wagner waiting on *her* response.

Unable to resist, she stretched the moment a little longer. "Perhaps you would care for a morning biscuit. I'm sure that Lydia wouldn't mind running back to Aunt Margaret's house to get one for you." Turning her most charming smile on her cousin, she added, "would you, Lydia?"

Waving his hand in mid-air, Mr. Wagner said, "Now there's no need to go to such trouble. I'm only going to be here for a few minutes."

Lydia fussed with her hair and leaned against the desk, while Mr. Wagner stood by the desk shifting his weight anxiously from one foot to the other.

"I've a message for Aunt Margaret."

"I see."

"Actually, this concerns Mr. Stanton." Turning, she faced him and found that he was leaning against the bars studying her.

"I've been talking with Alexander Judson. I don't know if you're aware of this, Mr. Stanton, but Mr. Judson owns the lumber mill."

"I didn't know that." Quirking an eyebrow, he asked, "Is there a reason why I should care about this?"

"As a matter of fact there is." Taking a step towards him, she couldn't hide her smile. "Mr. Judson has agreed to let you participate in Surprise's new work release program."

Silence descended on the room. When several moments passed and still no one spoke, she cleared her throat.

"It's a new idea. One that will benefit the town while at the same time keeping the prisoner under a watchful eye."

She looked over her shoulder at Lydia and Mr. Wagner. Lydia stood there smiling in that innocent way she had, while Mr. Wagner was pretending to study his fingernails.

Looking back at Mr. Stanton she was a bit surprised to find him staring at her. The expression on his face was hidden beneath the thick beard. If he were happy about the decision he wasn't saying. For a brief minute she thought she saw something in his eyes—a glimmer of hope perhaps? Then in the next instant his gaze was hooded once more.

Clearing her throat, she began. "Mr. Stanton, do you like the idea of a work release program?"

He seemed intent on staring at her. Feeling more than a little unnerved by this, she prodded, "Mr. Stanton?"

"You trust me enough not to run off?"

She blinked hard, his question startling her. But her answer startled her even more. Quietly, she replied, "Yes, I do trust you." And amazingly, Abigail did. Maybe it was the fact that when he'd been showing her how to handle a gun he didn't turn the weapon on her and escape right then and there. Or was it because something deep down inside of her knew he could do no harm? Whatever the reason was, Abigail knew in her heart he could be trusted.

"If you feel it's the right thing for your prisoner to be doing, then yes, I'd like to give it a try."

She felt herself smiling. "Great!"

"Exactly what will Mr. Stanton be doing?" Mr. Wagner wanted to know.

"Alexander Judson has agreed to Mr. Stanton's working for him at the lumber yard. He'll be helping to get the orders ready to deliver."

"I see you have this matter under control, Sheriff." John slapped his hands together, put his hat back on, and waited while she readied Mr. Stanton for his release.

Getting the key ring from the top desk drawer, she walked back to the cell, unlocking the door. "Mr. Stanton, you will be escorted over to the Judson lumber yard at eight o'clock every morning and then be brought back here by six o'clock each night."

Looking pointedly at John, she said, "You can let

Aunt Margaret know that I've settled all of the details with Mr. Judson."

"Yes."

"Good." Taking hold of Cole's arm she led him out the front door.

The sun was warm, a stark contrast to the coolness of the office. At mid-morning the town was alive with activity. It seemed that every few days more and more people were getting off the train and lingering in Surprise. Lydia had shown her the advertisement in the Albany paper and told her Aunt Margaret had placed it.

She didn't know what to think of this sudden population explosion, but she felt prepared to face anything.

They were just about at the entrance to the lumber yard when a woman, with the reddest hair that Abigail had ever seen, came hurrying across the street after them.

"Hello there, Cole!"

Abigail would have paused to let him stop and acknowledge the woman, but Cole just kept trudging along to their destination.

"Mr. Stanton, I think it would be rather rude to ignore the lady."

"She's no lady," he mumbled just loud enough for Abigail to hear.

"That's not a very nice thing to say." Abigail was

out and out curious about this woman who she knew to be Wanda McGurdy, formerly of Albany.

She managed to catch up to them. Narrowing her eyes, Abigail squinted at the woman. She was most certainly not a natural redhead. Furthermore, the dress she wore was more suited to evening attire, not the light of day. The neckline, scooped daringly low, was barely doing its job to conceal her bosom.

"Cole, I was on my way to visit you at the jail. Have they decided to let you go?"

"No."

Abigail jerked her head around to look at him after his gruff one-word answer. She wondered at the cause of his manner toward this woman? Since the two of them hadn't been introduced Abigail took it upon herself to do the honors.

"I'm Sheriff Abigail Monroe."

"Wanda McCurdy. Cole and I are old friends. We go way back." Wiggling her perfectly arched eyebrows, she added, "If you know what I mean?"

Stunned by this woman's boldness, Abigail simply stared at her.

"Cole hasn't mentioned me? I've been to visit him several times since his arrest. You and I kept missing each other I guess."

"Yes, well I do have a town to keep safe," Abigail replied, unable to keep from staring at the woman's cleavage.

It was easy to see why a man like Cole would be attracted to a woman like Miss McCurdy. She put her wares out there for the world to see without so much as batting an eye. Abigail wouldn't be caught dead in a dress like hers.

She stuck to the simple style because it suited her job. Still she couldn't help feeling much like she did the night she'd first arrested Cole Stanton. Inadequate. If only a dress could make her feel like holding a gun did—confident, powerful.

"Wanda . . . I mean, Miss McCurdy and I have known each other for several years. We are just acquaintances, nothing more."

Now, why, Abigail wondered, was Cole making such an effort to distance himself from Miss McCurdy when she so obviously wanted Abigail to think the two shared a past?

Chapter Eight

Deep down inside Cole had been hoping that the Sheriff and Wanda would never have met. But in a town this small he knew that would be impossible and was surprised it had taken this long for the two of them to run into each other.

Wanda McCurdy couldn't hold a candle to Abigail Monroe. Wanda was brash and bawdy, while Miss Abigail was very much the lady. Glancing at Abigail's face, Cole recognized the doubt shadowing her features. Even if she didn't realize it at this moment, Abigail had more class and manners in one little finger that Wanda did in her entire body.

He knew she had pluck and wanted her to show it now.

As if she'd read his mind, Abigail said, "Miss

McCurdy, I'm afraid that now isn't a good time for Mr. Stanton to have a visitor."

Wanda looked downright insulted by this turn of events. Cole knew she expected to be the center of attention in any situation that involved her.

"I see." Her face was flushed as her brown eyes flashed. Cole wanted to tell Wanda to put those claws of hers back in, but he figured the sheriff could hold her own in this battle.

Facing off against Abigail, she asked, "When do you suppose would be a good time for Mr. Stanton to have a visitor?"

"You can stop by the jail after dinner is served. Mr. Stanton is allowed one visitor before I lock up for the evening."

Wanda was a bit put out by the answer, then turned her back and stomped off in the direction of the mercantile.

Following the Sheriff into the shadows cast by the pole barn, he thought about how good if felt to be out of the cramped cell. He didn't care if this work release program was a bit unorthodox—it was refreshing to be outside.

A man dressed in blue work pants and a heavy cotton shirt with sleeves rolled up to his elbows walked towards them. Cole assumed he was the owner of the lumber yard.

"Howdy." He greeted them as if they were paying customers. "You must be Cole Stanton."

Cole nodded.

"I'm Alexander Judson. Right pleased to have you around to help out. Seems like there was nothing going on in this town for months on end, and now everybody wants to build something."

Removing his felt-brimmed hat, he rubbed his arm across his brow. "According to Miss Margaret and the Sheriff here, you're going to be here every day until the circuit judge comes along."

"That's right, Mr. Judson," Sheriff Abigail said.

Glancing out of the corner of his eye, Cole noticed that the Sheriff was getting all fired up. Her fists were clenched by her side and her lips were pursed together. If that didn't signal a female hankering for a fight, Cole didn't know what did. He sure was glad that he wasn't going to be the one on the receiving end of her wrath this time.

"Excuse me, Mr. Judson, did I hear correctly, you say you've spoken to my aunt about this?"

"Well Mr. Wagner came over on her behalf."

"Really."

He nodded and Cole was amused to no end to see Mr. Judson being the one who looked like he'd swallowed a sour grape.

"If you have everything under control, I'll just leave Mr. Stanton with you and come back this afternoon."

"That'll be fine, Sheriff."

Abigail was spitting mad at her aunt. She was going to get the matter of exactly who had control over the law in this town settled once and for all. Her brisk footsteps left small clouds of dust in their wake.

"Abigail! Wait for me."

Oh dear, in her haste to get home, she'd completely forgotten about Lydia. Slowing her steps, she waited for her cousin to catch up.

"What has gotten in to you?" Lydia puffed as she kept pace with Abigail.

"Aunt Margaret. She insists on my taking over as Sheriff and then she won't let me do my job. It's infuriating the way she controls this town."

Pushing back a stray lock of her red hair, Lydia suggested, "Perhaps she wants to make sure that you're safe."

As the mammoth house came in to full view, Abigail felt her anger cooling. "I can understand that, Lydia. In order for the people of this town to respect me, they have to be able to trust that I can make the right decisions when it comes to upholding the law. Right now, everyone seems to think Aunt Margaret came up with the idea to put Mr. Stanton on this work release program."

"Is that what you think, Lydia?" Her voice raised a half octave.

"Heavens, no!" Pausing on the steps leading to

the front porch, Lydia said, "Goodness, I'd no idea that you were taking this job so seriously."

"Of course I do, Lydia," Abigail scoffed. It was hard for her to admit, "This is the first time I've felt useful in ages. Edwin Quinn did his part months ago by taking the wind out of my sails, but no more. I enjoy this job."

Leading the way into the house, Lydia held the door open for her. Smiling, she patted Abigail's arm. "I can tell. I'm sorry about what happened between you and Edwin."

"Thank you." Squaring her shoulders, she added, "My broken engagement is a thing of the past. I'm starting my life anew right here in Surprise."

"I'm glad to hear you say those words." Aunt Margaret was in the grand hallway sitting in her wheelchair with Anna standing close by her side.

Without waiting a second longer, fearing she'd lose her courage, Abigail said, "Aunt Margaret, I need to have a few words with you."

Her aunt frowned. Abigail could see that she was trying hard to look contrite, but it wasn't going to work this time.

"This is about my interference in your work release program, isn't it?"

"Yes."

While Anna turned the wheelchair around and headed back into the front sitting room, Abigail and Lydia exchanged worried glances.

"Come in and sit, girls. Anna will bring us some tea and cookies," Aunt Margaret said, as if tea and cookies could solve the world's problems.

With her aunt's wheelchair positioned in front of the fireplace, Abigail chose to sit across from her on a small overstuffed rose-colored chintz covered sofa; Lydia perched herself on the edge of a matching wing-back chair.

It seemed that all eyes were turned towards her. Looking from her aunt's watery blue eyes, to Lydia's green ones, she cleared her throat purposely.

"I know you mean well, Aunt Margaret. Don't get me wrong, but the work release program was my idea."

"But—" her aunt started.

"I don't like the way you and Mr. Wagner keep trying to control my job without my knowledge. I want it to stop, right now."

"All right, dear."

Blinking in surprise at how easily she'd just given in to her request, Abigail managed a shaky smile. "You don't mind?"

"You are the sheriff, dear."

Oh, something was fishy here. Aunt Margaret was a stubborn woman who liked to have everything go her way and she very rarely if ever, gave in. Abigail looked to Lydia for some guidance and all she did was shrug her delicate shoulders as she met Abigail's stare.

"So tell me, how did Mr. Stanton react to his circumstances?"

"He seemed fine with the idea of being out of jail. I've set the schedule for his work release time and everyone, including Mr. Judson, seems happy."

Anna wheeled the mahogany tea cart into the room. She poured out three cups of steaming tea, and then picking up the silver serving tongs, placed a delicate sugar cookie on the plate beside each cup.

Accepting her tea and cookie, Lydia said, "Mr. Stanton may be in a bit of trouble, but he seems like a fine gentleman to me."

"I have to agree, Lydia. He's been here for Sunday dinner twice now, and has always been a gracious guest. He's well mannered; granted, his using a bit of shaving cream and a sharp razor wouldn't hurt."

What was it about Cole Stanton that left these women besotted with him? Their conversation continued as if she weren't even in the room. Forcing herself to chew and swallow the now tasteless cookie, Abigail waited for her temper to cool.

"I could stop by Mr. Jules' store and pick up a shaving kit for him." That Lydia had the nerve to suggest doing such a thing infuriated Abigail all over again.

Sipping her tea, Aunt Margaret glanced at Abigail over the rim of the fragile china cup. "What do you think, Abigail?"

Studying her aunt for a full minute, and not finding any sign that she was just being condescending, Abigail formed her answer slowly, deliberately. "I suppose Mr. Stanton would be grateful for the opportunity to neaten himself up a bit."

"And what of his clothing, Abigail?" Lydia persisted with her questions.

"What of it?" she spat out. Aunt Margaret raised her eyebrows in disapproval.

"I heard his bags were stolen right out from underneath him when he was traveling on the train. He could use an extra set of clothing now that he's going to be working. Honestly, Abigail, you've no idea how long he's going to be incarcerated. If it's the town's responsibility to feed and house him, then it should also be our responsibility to supply him with clothing."

In all the time that she'd missed seeing her cousin Lydia, Abigail realized that she hadn't missed how opinionated the young woman could be. However, she did raise a good point. Mr. Stanton would need clothing. "We will give him two pairs of pants, two shirts, undergarments and nothing more. Do you understand me, Aunt Margaret? Lydia?"

Satisfied when both women nodded to her, she set down her tea cup and saucer, gathered her wits about her, and prepared to go back to town where she hoped to get some real work accomplished. There was the filing and posting of the Wanted posters and she had to get a fresh change of linens on the cot in the jail cell before Mr. Stanton returned for the evening.

Her aunt's and cousin's conversation flowed around her while she made a mental list of everything she wanted to get done before sundown. They discussed dinner menus and the latest clothing styles, but it wasn't until she heard Cole Stanton's name that she swung her attention back to them.

"What's this about Mr. Stanton?"

"I think he's rather handsome and I don't think he's capable of committing the crime that you've arrested him for."

Her mouth dropped open at Lydia's comment. It couldn't be helped, she was shocked by her declaration. "Lydia, you hardly know the man," Abigail quickly reminded her. "And furthermore, I had no choice but to arrest him. He fit the description on the Wanted poster perfectly."

"Perhaps it's a case of mistaken identity," Aunt Margaret suggested.

She turned that thought over in her mind. It was a possibility she hadn't considered. The fact remained that Cole Stanton fit the description and there was no arguing around the issue.

"Did you even think to ask him if he was innocent?"

She shook her head in response to Lydia's question. Even if, ever so briefly, the thought had occurred to her, the fact remained that it wasn't her job to decide such a thing.

Raising her eyebrows, Aunt Margaret asked, "Well, Abigail, do *you* think he committed the robbery?"

Chapter Nine

Abigail didn't want to think about the question, or her answer, right now. "I have to get back to work." Rising from the sofa, she straightened her skirt, nervously brushing cookie crumbs from the sturdy cotton fabric.

"Thank you for the tea, Aunt Margaret." Looking to her cousin, she smiled and said, "Enjoy the rest of your morning, Lydia."

"You too," Lydia chirped, a bit too cheerfully.

Even though the sun was shining, Abigail didn't feel there was much joy left in her day. Walking from the house, Abigail found her thoughts churning like a whirlpool. The question posed by her aunt was troubling. It disturbed her to consider she might have an innocent man in jail; as much as she was loathe to admit it, the possibility existed.

Shaking the uncertainties from her mind, she strolled past the site where the new school was going to be built. Long wooden surveyor stakes stuck into the earth marked the perimeter of the future building.

Nearing Judson's lumber yard she could smell the scent of fresh cut wood. Alexander Judson was a fine man who'd been a widower for going on three years now. With a young son and daughter to support, the extra help would mean he could take on more work and not have to pay for it.

"Hey, you little scamps! Come back here with my hat!"

Though she didn't see who was yelling, Abigail managed to round the corner of the lumber mill just in time to see two boys running at full speed across the street. She knew just how to head them off. Running across the street, she quickly skirted around the mercantile and cut the boys off at the pass, so to speak.

"James Macintyre and Matthew Duncan, haven't you boys been in enough trouble lately?" she scolded.

"Aw, come on, Sheriff. Let us go. We didn't do nuttin' wrong."

She held a squirming James firmly by the scruff

of his neck. "Yes, you did. Now where did you get that hat from?"

"We found it on the ground," Matthew chimed in answer.

While she held onto James, Matthew was busy fidgeting around in front of her. Scuffing his feet around the dirt and screwing up his face, trying to look either mean or innocent, Abigail couldn't tell which.

"Yeah! Finders keepers," James said with a gleeful smile.

"That's right, we found it so now it's ours." Matthew stabbed his finger in her direction, punctuating each word with a thrust of his hand.

Looking down at the ladies hat, that in a few more minutes would surely have been ruined beyond repair, she began to develop a punishment for the boys; hopefully, one that they soon wouldn't forget.

"So, you think the hat should belong to you, James?"

He nodded fiercely.

She smiled ever so sweetly at the two urchins. They had no idea what was coming and were probably thinking that she was going to let them go. Well, they would be wrong.

She continued smiling and said, "Let's see how it looks on you."

"You want me to put it on *my head*?"

"I sure do. And then we can see how it looks on Matthew."

"I can't do that, Sheriff. What if somebody sees me?"

"You should have thought of that before you stole it from the lady." Releasing her hold on him, she placed her hands on her hips, ordering, "Put the hat on."

His little Adam's apple bobbed up and down as he swallowed. She felt sorry for the little scamps, but it was their doing that had gotten them in this mess in the first place.

Slowly he placed on his head the floppy hat with the bright pink dried flowers adorning the brim.

"Now turn around and show Matthew how it looks."

James did as he was told while his friend howled with laughter.

"I wouldn't be so happy if I were you. You're next." Lifting the hat from James' crop of blond hair, she gave the bonnet to Matthew. "Your turn."

He shook his head. "I'm not putting that ugly thing on."

"Come along then." Taking hold of his skinny arm, she started to lead him around the front of the building.

"Where are you taking me?" His bottom lip quivered.

"To jail," she answered sternly. "If you don't want to wear that hat and show James how you look in it, then you can sit in my jail cell for the rest of the day."

"Put the hat on Matt. It's just me and her that's going to see you," his friend cajoled.

"I ain't wearing no lady's hat!"

"Your pa is going to be mighty mad at you when he has to come get you out of jail."

She had to hand it to James, he was trying his darndest to keep his pal out of trouble. Matthew's being stubborn made her wonder just how long he planned on holding out.

Abigail helped his decision along, saying, "You can run along home now, James. Matthew will be spending the rest of the day in jail."

The boy dug his heels into the ground. "I've changed my mind, Sheriff Abigail. Give me the stupid hat."

Obliging him, she handed him the ruined bonnet and watched, barely containing her amusement as he paraded around in front of his friend. After a few torturous minutes she took the hat from him.

"Boys, you run along now and stay out of trouble. The next time I catch you up to no good I'm going to speak with your parents."

The two were around the building before she could finish her sentence. Still carrying the hat, Abigail went in search of its owner. It didn't take her long to figure out who it belonged to.

Wanda McCurdy and her pile of dyed red hair sidled up so close to Mr. Stanton that Abigail couldn't tell where he ended and she began.

"Cole, those two rascals stole my hat. They snatched it right out from my hand." Miss McCurdy was busy batting her long lashes at Cole and didn't seem to notice Abigail, who was now standing a mere two feet away from them.

Abigail cleared her throat and the woman turned to look down her nose at her. She noticed right away that Miss McCurdy had added a few accessories to her wardrobe. Pretty earrings dangled from her ear lobes, and upon closer inspection of the hat, Abigail decided that it wasn't your run of the mill simple dime store version. The ribbon was a fine satin and the label inside the brim indicated the bonnet came from a fine haberdashery in Albany.

She couldn't help thinking how interesting it was the way the clothes didn't seem to fit the woman.

"Oh, Sheriff, I see you've found my hat." Taking the hat from her without so much as a thank you, she continued on, "I hope those two boys are being punished."

She'd barely heard what Miss McCurdy was saying. Cole was standing there with his shirtsleeves rolled up to his elbows and a thin sheen of perspiration covering his forehead. He looked as if he'd been working hard. He also looked mighty handsome.

"Sheriff? Did you punish those boys?" Miss McCurdy persisted.

"I sent them both home with a warning," Abigail answered.

"Good," Miss McCurdy sniffed. Turning her round eyes towards Cole, she said, "I've brought you a picnic lunch. You must be famished after all these long hours of work." Reaching out, she ran a hand over his brow. "Look at you just dripping with sweat."

Abigail fairly quaked in her shoes at the bold audacity of this woman. The nerve of her to be so boldly touching Mr. Stanton in such an intimate way! He fixed his gaze on her.

"I am allowed to eat while I'm doing my penance, aren't I?"

Abigail swallowed her unwanted and unexpected feelings of jealousy. "You can take a break for lunch if it's all right with Mr. Judson."

Turning his head, Mr. Stanton bellowed, "Alex! Is it time for our lunch break?"

Alex? He was already calling Alexander Judson by his given name? Why the day wasn't even half over yet and already he was on familiar terms with his boss. What was it about this man that made everyone in this town want to be his friend, while she so wanted to dislike him?

From in the back of the shop came the mill owner's reply that Cole could take a half-hour lunch break.

"You have to stay within sight of the building, Mr. Stanton." Abigail threw her shoulders back and stood tall, falling back into her sheriff mode.

"We'll be sure to do just that, Sheriff." Taking Miss McCurdy by the elbow, Cole guided her over to a bench under the inviting shade of a big oak tree that sat in the center of town.

Great, just great, Abigail thought, now everyone would see Mr. Stanton having lunch with that woman. Infuriated with herself for even caring, Abigail walked back to the office. She had work to do and the less she saw of the couple the better!

Beneath his beard, Cole grinned. Abigail sure was in a huff over him spending time with Wanda. He enjoyed her reaction to seeing the two of them together. The way the pink blush tinged her cheeks was a sight to behold. He never would have guessed that she'd be one to fall into the old green-eyed monster trap. But it appeared she had and he was glad of it. The sheriff had a soft spot for him; even if she didn't care to admit it.

"Cole, would you like to try some of this baked chicken?" Wanda lifted the lid off a square tin revealing the fragrant meat.

"Don't mind if I do." He was never one to turn

down home cooking, even if it was being offered by a she-devil. Winking at her, Cole helped himself to a chicken leg.

Taking a big healthy bite, he marveled at the tenderness and flavor of the meat, savoring every bit of it. Finishing off the last of the piece, he tossed the bone in the grass and turned his attention to the woman sitting next to him. Wanda McCurdy was up to something and Cole had this itching feeling at the base of his neck that it involved him.

He'd had a lot of time to think while being locked up, and several bits of information concerning his arrest weren't adding up. Oh, the description on the Wanted poster fit him all right and he had been in Albany the week the jewelry store was robbed, however, that was where the similarities ended.

The more interesting fact was Wanda being in Albany at the same time. While he'd traveled around a lot over the years, and letting his hair grow out may have made him look like a criminal, he wasn't. He'd a bad feeling about Wanda McCurdy. She very well could have something to do with the theft. Was it really a coincidence the way she just happened to turn up in Surprise?

Cole was going to have to prove his innocence and Wanda was the key. Turning his head, he looked at her, and sent her what was surely one of his most charming smiles.

"So how are you enjoying Surprise?"

"It's an interesting little town." Adjusting the ties on her bonnet, she fixed it on top of her mass of red hair. "More interesting because I found you here."

"Umm. Except I'm here because I can't leave." Shrugging, he added, "You know the pesky little problem I have of being incarcerated?"

"Yes, it is dreadful. I can't believe that woman sheriff can possibly think you are capable of such a thing." She paused, pursing her full lips together and then said, "I can't believe the sheriff is a woman."

"Me neither," Cole quietly admitted.

While Wanda was distracted by her bonnet, Cole looked at her. She was wearing a dress looking like the latest style. The fabric was shiny and new, with nary a wrinkle or stain to be found. And while he thought the hat she was so obsessed with seemed frivolous, upon closer inspection he noticed that it, too, appeared new and wondered if she'd purchased it from a fine haberdashery.

From what he knew about her, Cole thought it improbable that she was able to afford such fineries. It was clear that she'd come to Surprise alone. So it was safe to assume that she didn't have a man escorting her. He thought for a minute on how many months had passed since they'd parted ways and guessed that it was no more than four.

Then, she'd been just another saloon girl with no

family to speak of. There was no way she'd earned enough to buy expensive clothes. When and how had she come into so much money?

"Cole?" Her seductive tone broke through his thoughts.

He found her staring at him with an inviting look in her eyes. "Yes, Wanda."

"Do you like my new dress?" She nudged closer to him, their hips bumping together.

He could smell her expensive perfume. "What's the occasion?"

"I think having lunch with you is occasion enough to wear something special."

"Did you buy the dress just to wear it in this one-horse town?"

"No. I purchased it in Albany. You remember that lovely shop on Quail Street? The one on the corner, we used to stroll by on our afternoon walks." She reached out and, laying her hand across his chest, began to finger his shirt buttons.

Taking her hand in his, he pulled it down to his side. "Wanda, while I like your attention, I don't think this is the time or the place to be carrying on."

She looked around then, as if she were startled to find they were sitting out in the open. "Yes, you're right. We wouldn't want to set any more tongues wagging now would we?"

Cole thought they'd probably already done that, seeing how they were sitting under the biggest shade tree in the center of town in clear view. Wives were going about their daily chores while their husbands worked the fields. Behind him he could hear the saws from Judson's lumber yard buzzing through lengths of tree trunks.

In front of him the town sat in two neat rows of buildings. And aiming straight for him, with purpose in every step, was Sheriff Abigail Monroe.

Chapter Ten

He noticed right away she wasn't smiling. Then he remembered he'd rarely seen her smile. Too bad, she'd such a lovely mouth, one made for smiling and just maybe a little kissing. Preparing for her angry onslaught, he stood bracing his feet apart.

Holding her pocket watch in her hand, Abigail studied it for a moment, looked to the sky as if checking the sun's position and said, "Mr. Stanton, I believe it's time for you to be back at work."

He so wanted to smile at her, but deliberately kept a straight face. "I was just heading that way." Nodding at Wanda, he thanked her for the lunch. "Miss McCurdy, lunch was delicious. Thank you for bringing it by."

"You're very welcome, Cole." Packing up the

remnants of their lunch, she turned to Abigail. "Good day, Sheriff." With a quick turn and a flounce of her skirts, she was off.

A warm breeze fanned Abigail's skirts. Such a nice figure for a sheriff, he thought. She was watching Wanda with her brow furrowed together in deep concentration. Cole would have given anything to know what her thoughts were, but didn't dare ask.

Their relationship was tenuous at best.

Her head snapped around and she glared at him. He raised his hands in self-defense. "Hey, don't look at me like that."

"I assume that the two of you are old friends."

Starting to walk back to work, he waited for her steps to fall beside him before commenting. "Wanda and I met in Albany. She was serving drinks at a local saloon."

"I see," she replied, nibbling on her lower lip contemplatively.

"No, you don't." He wasn't about to explain his relationship with Wanda to her. There really was nothing to say, even if he wanted Wanda and maybe Abigail thinking there was.

Raising her eyes to look at him, she said, "Yes, I do. Let me ask you a question, Mr. Stanton. How does a saloon girl come up with enough money to pay for such finery?"

With a quick shrug of his shoulders, he replied,

"I don't know." He needed to prove his innocence and Wanda was the only one who could help him do that. He didn't trust Abigail with the truth. After all she was the one who'd chased him down and arrested him. He wasn't sure just how far she'd go to uphold the law. Cole could be sitting in the jail until next year.

As much as Abigail's company was growing on him, he didn't think he could last out much longer being locked up in that tiny jail cell. Something was going to have to be done and soon!

"I suspect she didn't come by her money in an honest way."

As they entered the dusty interior of the lumber mill, Cole mulled over her observation. Could it be possible that the sheriff was thinking along the same lines as he was—Miss McCurdy was hiding something?

Then just like a snap of the fingers, as if the conversation they were having never happened, the sheriff turned to him and asked, "What size pants do you wear?"

"I beg your pardon?" What was she up to now, he wondered, placing his hands on his hips as he stared down at her.

"I'll need your shirt size also."

There she was all prim and proper asking him personal questions. Shrugging his shoulders, Cole

decided her asking was just another one of the odd-
ities of this town. Not sure where all this would land
him, reluctantly he gave her the information.

"Can I get back to work now?"

"Yes, you may."

The afternoon gave Abigail some much needed
time to think. At first she'd been so rattled by seeing
Cole with that horrible woman she'd barely been
able to concentrate. Then the thought dawned on
her; if Cole was as innocent as he professed to be,
Miss McCurdy could very well hold the key to his
freedom.

As she shopped for his clothing, she began to
formulate a plan. Abigail instructed Mr. Jules to put
the items on her aunt's account and told him that if
Lydia showed up, to let her know the purchases had
been made.

With the task completed, she stood back looking
at the items laid out neatly on the cot and admired
the choices she'd made. Two shirts, one a durable
blue cotton material and the other white, so that he
could wear it to the Sunday dinners that Aunt Margaret still insisted on having. The trousers had been
purchased with the same idea in mind, one pair durable and the other a bit dressier.

She'd set the shaving kit on a small stand near
the cot, alongside a white porcelain bowl and

pitcher. Abigail tried to imagine what Cole would look like with all that hair shaved off, and couldn't.

Returning to her desk, she set about putting it in order. She was placing the pile of Wanted posters in the top drawer when her gaze fell upon the one with Cole Stanton's description. Rubbing her hands up and down her arms, she wondered again if she might have acted too hastily in arresting him. Once again after studying the paper, she decided he did indeed fit the description.

The door opened letting in a warm afternoon breeze and her prisoner. Her stomach fluttered at the sight of him filling the space in the doorway. Abigail wondered at her reaction to him and wished that she could stop it from happening. She'd no business being attracted to such a man.

After all, she was the sheriff and he was a prisoner for goodness sakes! For propriety's sake alone she had to stop this.

"What's for dinner, sweetheart?" Cole drawled, closing the door behind him.

Through clenched teeth and a jaw set hard as granite, she said, "I'm not your sweetheart!" For an instant Abigail thought he'd lost his mind and then she saw the grin beneath his thick beard and realized he was joking. Ignoring his good humor, she shuffled some papers around the desk, determined not to smile back at him.

"I take it you enjoyed the work at the lumber mill?"

"I did." He sauntered across the room towards the cell like he hadn't a care in the world.

She held her breath, for surely by now he'd noticed the items lying on top of the cot. Silence filled the room while she waited for his reaction. It wasn't that long of a wait.

"Sheriff, would you mind stepping over here for a minute?"

Nibbling her lower lip, she stood up and slowly made her way over to him. "Is there a problem, Mr. Stanton?"

He turned so quickly that Abigail was forced off balance. She stumbled against the steel bars, catching herself. His dark eyes widened.

"Yes, there's a problem!" he barked.

He stood toe-to-toe with her, so close she could feel the heat coming off his body. It penetrated her clothing, making her feel a tad uncomfortable.

"There's no need to yell, Mr. Stanton."

The skin about his beard reddened. He swallowed and then said, in a softer tone, "What is the meaning of this?" He pointed an accusing finger towards the cot.

"You mean the pants and shirts?"

"Stop acting coy." Hands on his hips he was looking down at her.

Coy? He thought she was acting coy? Abigail didn't think she possessed a coy bone in her body, but come to think of it she rather liked the idea of being coy.

Folding her arms, she countered with, "What did you think I needed your pants and shirt size for, if not to buy you some?"

"Don't you think it's a bit personal to be buying clothing for a man that you barely know?"

"Really, Mr. Stanton, it seemed the proper thing to do. You've been traipsing around in the same clothes for as long as you've been here. I didn't see your traveling bag."

He smirked at her. "For your information, my clothing bag was stolen."

"Hmm. Yes, I do remember someone mentioning that to me."

"Would that someone happen to be your cousin Lydia?"

"As a matter of fact, yes it was."

"Miss Lydia seems to know an awful lot of what goes on around here. She's spunky."

It was one thing to have to contend with his feelings about Miss Wanda McCurdy, but quite another to have him saying such a thing about her cousin. "I was the one who picked them out," Abigail said before she could stop herself.

She didn't like thinking how much she'd enjoyed

picking out clothes for him. It was hard enough knowing it mattered Mr. Stanton knew she'd been the one to do it.

There you had it though, in as much as she shouldn't care one way or the other, Abigail wanted to please this man.

He smiled at her remark; a slow languid smile that reached his eyes. "Thank you."

"You're welcome."

"I'll pay you back once I'm free and working for pay."

"There's no need to do that. Aunt Margaret is taking care of everything."

"Tell her, I'll pay her back." He turned to pick up the white dress shirt and black pants.

Abigail sensed his pride was at stake and acquiesced. "I'll let her know." Several minutes passed before he saw the shaving kit.

"Growing tired of my beard?" he asked, looking over his shoulder at her.

Sucking her lower lip between her teeth, Abigail wondered what he looked like for real, without all the dark locks of thick hair.

His voice was low when he spoke. "You don't have to say a word, the answer is written all over your face."

"We were just giving you options, Mr. Stanton."

"Hmm, no doubt that was Lydia's idea again."

"Yes. But—"

"I know, I know," he interrupted, "you were the one who picked it out."

Actually, Mr. Jules picked the items out and Abigail didn't see any need for Mr. Stanton to be made aware of that.

"I'll need some hot water."

It was a full minute before she realized what he was implying. Stunned by his quick decision, she asked, "You're really going to shave the beard off?"

"I am. Now hurry up and bring me some hot water before I change my mind," he said with a smile.

Abigail left the cell and went to the stove where a low fire was kept burning to keep her tea water warm. Picking up the copper kettle, she carried it to the cell and poured the steaming water into the washbowl.

"Thank you." Cole was unbuttoning his work shirt when Abigail turned around.

Feeling flustered, she said, "I'll just leave you."

Before she could go, he reached out and laid his hand on her wrist, stopping her. "Just one more thing, Sheriff—you and I need to strike a bargain."

His long fingers closed gently around her wrist. Her flesh felt on fire from his touch. "A bargain?" she squeaked.

He laughed. "Yes. If I'm to accept the clothes and shaving kit *and* actually use the razor, then you have to agree to start calling me by my first name and allow me to do the same for you. Another thing, let's be civil. I'm not such a bad person."

She searched his eyes for any sign of who he really was. Whether or not he was a bad person remained to be seen.

"You want me to call you Cole and you're to call me Abigail, and you'll shave off your beard for that?"

"Correct."

What harm could there be in accepting his terms? They were together for a fair amount of their days anyway. But if she stopped calling him Mr. Stanton then he might not respect her authority. Abigail wasn't sure what to do.

"If I let you call me by my given name will you still respect me as the sheriff?"

"Yes." He gave her wrist a quick squeeze, which she was certain was meant to encourage her, but it had quite a different effect altogether.

The heat from his touch sent her pulse racing so she thought she might swoon. Abigail had to leave before she made a fool out of herself. "You have a deal, Mr. Stanton." She hoped her voice didn't sound as breathy as she felt.

He raised his eyebrows.

"I meant to say, Cole."

"Thank you, Abigail."

Hearing her name come from his lips sent shivers

racing down her spine. Never in all the time she'd spent courting Edwin did she ever feel like this. Come to think of it, near the end of their relationship the only thing she'd felt when he called to her, was dread.

This was a far better feeling. She smiled.

"You should do that more often."

"What?"

Releasing her hand, he reached up and ran his thumb across her lips. "Smile."

If she thought his touch jolted her before, this time she fairly jumped out of her skin. Clearing her throat she said softly, "I should let you get to your shaving."

Dropping his hand to his side, he nodded in agreement.

Turning, she left the cell. "I'll be just outside the door. If you need anything just give a shout."

"I'll be sure and do just that."

He was grinning at her, she was sure of it. But Abigail didn't dare look back to see. Instead, she opened the door to the office and went outside for a welcoming breath of fresh air. The sun felt warm for the first time in a long while.

The minutes seemed to crawl by. Abigail started to pace along the walkway in front of the building. Back and forth she went, in carefully measured steps. Every once in a while she'd pause to peer through the windows. The dust had built up on the glass again making it near impossible to see what he, *Cole*, was doing.

She began to tap her toe, impatient with the process. After a few minutes she went back to pacing again—one long measured step after another. When three quarters of an hour had passed and still no sound from within, Abigail decided it was time to see exactly what was going on.

The brass knob felt cold against her palm. Slowly she turned it, pushing the door open. Cole was sitting on the edge of the cot. And as Abigail looked at him, the breath left her body. She gripped the doorknob to keep from fainting at the sight of him.

"Oh, my . . ." she gasped. What had she done?

Chapter Eleven

Stepping into the room, Abigail thought her heart might just stop beating at the sight of him. She couldn't help thinking there ought to be a law against looking the way Cole Stanton did right now. Not only had he shaved his beard, but he'd changed out of his work clothes and into the white shirt and black trousers.

Even though he looked mighty fine in the new clothes, it was his face that held her mesmerized. Without his beard, the color of Cole's eyes appeared to be even darker, almost black. He'd high cheek-bones, and the line of his jaw was firm, strong. Her gaze traveled to his mouth, his full lips and she realized with a start that he was grinning rather sheepishly at her.

"Quite a change, huh?"

He was holding the cracked mirror that used to hang on the wall in his hand, looking at his reflection.

She was speechless.

He ran his free hand through the shortened locks of his dark hair. He'd cut his hair. The strands curled at the ends in soft waves.

And still she was speechless.

"Sheriff?" He arched his dark eyebrows, looking directly at her, waiting.

Clearing her throat, she swallowed hard. "You look . . . different." Now that was as lame a statement as she'd ever spoken.

"Different?"

Oh my. Whereas before she'd had to guess what he was thinking, now she could see it written clearly on his face. Narrowing his eyes, he gazed at her, looking befuddled.

Tossing the mirror onto the cot, he stood, placing his hand on his hips, he towered over her. "Is that the best you can come up with?" There was a devilish glint in his dark eyes.

"N-no," she stuttered. Taking a step back, she tried to fend him off. He matched her with a step of his own, pinning her against the steel bars.

"I know I look different. But, tell me, Abigail how do I really look to you now?" Along with the devilish glint he'd added a wolfish grin.

Devastating, dangerous, and those were just two of the words that began with D that she could think of off the top of her head.

"You look incredibly handsome." She said it so softly that Abigail wasn't sure she'd even spoken.

And then Cole grinned. "Thank you."

"My, my, my! Will you look at our prisoner now?" Lydia came sweeping into the office slamming the door behind her. "I went over to the mercantile to purchase some things and Mr. Jules informed me you'd already been in." She glanced quickly at Abigail.

Coming to stand just outside of the cell, she gave him a quick once over. "Mr. Stanton, you look like a new man. Oh, and by the way, I'm to extend an invitation for dinner to you. Aunt Margaret would like you to come this evening. That's if it's all right with the Sheriff."

"It's not Sunday," Cole said.

"Well, no it's not. I believe this is Wednesday. Aunt Margaret would like to know how the work release program is going."

Still stunned by the change in Cole's appearance, Abigail was only half-listening to what her cousin was saying. Nodding her head, she agreed to the dinner arrangements.

"Now that we have that settled, I'm to tell you, Mr. Wagner will be by to bring you to Aunt Margaret's in an hour." Grabbing hold of Abigail's arm,

Lydia tugged her out of the cell. "That will give us plenty of time to get ready."

Blinking, Abigail realized, too late, she'd agreed to yet another one of Aunt Margaret's ludicrous schemes. By the time they were outside and walking to the house, she knew there was to be no turning back.

"What are you two up to now?" She hated to sound cynical, but how could she help it, when the two of them continued to make plans without consulting her first.

Shrugging her delicate shoulders, Lydia replied, "Not a thing. This is just a dinner, Abigail. Why must you make it seem like something more?"

"Perhaps if you and our aunt saw fit to discuss these matters with me first I wouldn't always be put in the position of imagining the worst."

Lydia stopped walking and turned to face her. Abigail could see by the expression on her face she'd hurt her feelings.

"Have we ever done anything to hurt you, Abigail?"

Reaching out she pulled Lydia into her arms. "No and I'm sorry." Quick to reassure her she added, "I know you only want what's best for me."

"Yes, I do," Lydia sniffed more for effect.

Arm in arm they walked up the steps to the house. Anna met them at the door. "There you girls are. We were wondering what was keeping you.

Abigail, you're to go straight upstairs and change out of those clothes. Lydia, Miss Margaret needs your help in the dining room."

Both of them did as they were told. As Abigail made her way up the grand staircase to her room, she overheard Lydia saying to Aunt Margaret, "Mr. Stanton looks divine. Wait until you see him."

A smile tugged at the corners of her mouth and she gave into the feeling, thinking that divine was yet another word beginning with D. She hadn't thought of that word to describe Cole.

Abigail began to undress the moment she closed the bedroom door. Only when she was standing in her thin cotton chemise did she begin to panic. What on earth was she thinking? She was certain not one item in her wardrobe would be right for this evening.

She wanted to look as special as Cole did, but most of her clothing was brown or gray in color. Abigail wanted to wear something soft and feminine. Pushing one hanger after another to the back of her closet in frustration, Abigail was beginning to think all was lost when, with one last swish of dark fabric, a cream-colored gown was exposed.

Fingering the soft, satiny material, she tried not to remember the reason she'd purchased this particular gown. This was to have been part of her wedding trousseau. When she'd first come to Surprise she'd purposely hung the gown in the back of the closet where she wouldn't have to be reminded of the philandering Edwin Quinn.

Carefully, pulling the dress out, Abigail held the swirling garment up against her. This would be perfect for dinner.

She was preparing to finish dressing when a knock sounded at the door.

"Abigail, it's Lydia. May I come in?"

"By all means." Abigail threw the wrapper around her shoulders and ran to let her cousin in. And there, bless her heart, stood Lydia with a hairbrush and ribbons of varying colors and shades to dress Abigail's hair.

Lydia entered the room, the expression on her face bursting into a wide smile. "This is one of the prettiest dresses I've ever seen!" Placing the brush and ribbons on the low dressing table, she reached for the garment.

Fingering the soft and satiny fabric, Abigail beamed at Lydia. "It is perfect, isn't it? Help me get into this."

Twenty minutes later Lydia had not only helped her get into the pretty dress, but she'd also brushed out her hair and put it in a simple single braid that hung down Abigail's back. Standing in front of the Cheval mirror, they admired their handiwork.

"Not too over done and certainly not as drab as your sheriff's clothes. You look beautiful."

Staring at her reflection, Abigail thought she could agree with her cousin on this matter. Her transformation, while not as dramatic as Cole's, would certainly garner his attention. "Thank you for helping me."

Abigail couldn't help grinning at her. She knew that Lydia meant well by her comment, and truth be told, her daytime clothes were a tad bit drab. She was the Sheriff after all and couldn't very well be going around dressed like a floozy or heaven forbid, like Wanda McCurdy.

They left the room and went downstairs, where Anna was rushing to open the front door and usher in their dinner guests. Mr. Wagner entered ahead of Cole. Abigail paused, her foot just about to come off the last step.

Cole looked even better outside of the jail cell. Prisoner or not, the man simply took her breath away. It didn't take her long to notice that he was staring back at her. She'd almost forgotten about her own transformation.

"Sheriff, might I say, you're looking mighty pretty this evening."

"Thank you, Cole." Abigail smiled.

"You're welcome." He held his arm out, escorting her into the dining room where Aunt Margaret was seated at the head of the table.

"John, Mr. Stanton, I'm so glad you could both

join us." Aunt Margaret tilted her cheek expectantly. Leaning down Mr. Wagner placed a light kiss upon it.

A long row of tapered white candles sat snugly in brass holders lining the mantle, the flickering of the tiny flames casting a welcome glow over the room.

Looking over at the young woman being escorted on his arm, Cole considered Abigail. It was hard for him to believe that just a few short weeks ago he'd actually thought she was a weakling. Now it was quite clear to him just how mistaken he'd been. She was stronger in spirit than her cousin and aunt combined.

This evening she was especially pretty. He found himself flattered and humbled by the trouble she'd gone to for this evening's dinner. The cream-colored gown that she wore suited her. The garment hugged her curves in all the right places with the scooped neckline giving only a hint of the creamy white skin that lay beneath.

Her hair was done in a simple braid, a style that he found absolutely charming and beguiling on her at the same time. She smiled at him and he returned the favor.

"Mr. Stanton, you're looking very handsome this evening." Nodding at Abigail, Miss Margaret said,

"And you my dear, did a fine job of picking out his clothing."

The faintest of blushes rose on her face. Shrugging her shoulders, Abigail replied, "It was no trouble, really. Mr. Jules helped with most of the selections."

Uncomfortable at all the attention, Cole quickly changed the subject. "Thank you for the dinner invitation. And here I thought having prisoners at the table was only a Sunday tradition." He grinned at Miss Margaret.

He was going to miss his beard; the whiskers had done a fine job of hiding his expressions. Absently, rubbing a hand over the smooth skin, he felt naked.

"You're always welcome at my table."

Behind him, Abigail cleared her throat and he didn't have to turn around to know she was casting the severest of reprimanding looks at her aunt. The Sheriff didn't approve of all this nonsense. Well, what's done was done and no matter what, he was going to enjoy this heavenly prepared meal.

Two hours later they were all sitting in the formal front parlor enjoying a fine cup of coffee and a delicious chocolate cake. Even if this was the strangest town he'd ever been in, Cole would never regret his time spent having dinner with Miss Margaret.

"So tell me, Mr. Stanton, how do you know Wanda McCurdy?" Miss Margaret asked.

He concentrated on forcing every muscle in his face to remain still. Then taking a deep breath he answered, "I met her when I was in Albany."

The old woman innocently sipped at her tea, then smiled at him. "It's quite odd how she ended up here, isn't it?"

It didn't take long for Abigail to spring into action. "Aunt Margaret that will be enough," she warned.

"Really, Abigail, I'm just asking a question."

"The answers to which don't concern you."

Miss Margaret's eyes flashed in rare anger. "They most certainly do! If the citizens of this town are in any danger from that woman then it's my concern and yours as well, might I add."

Cole looked at her. It was amazing to think that when he'd first met her she seemed to be nothing more than a frail old woman on the brink of being bedridden. And now she had enough fire in her to heat the entire house. This only confirmed his suspicions—she was not ill.

It appeared that he wasn't the only in this town keeping secrets from the sheriff.

Lydia moved between her aunt and cousin. "Please don't argue. It will ruin a perfectly fine evening."

"For goodness sakes Lydia, Abigail and I are not arguing, we're having a heated exchange of words."

At Miss Margaret's comment the entire room

burst into laughter. Cole shook his head in disbelief thinking, this was one crazy family.

"What do you say I take Mr. Stanton back to jail and you can stay here, Sheriff?" Mr. Wagner asked.

Abigail snapped to attention. "He's my responsibility. I'll see he gets back safely. Thank you for the offer."

Mr. Wagner smiled that goofy smile of his and said, "Goodnight then. Margaret, thank you for a delightful evening and as always the food was delicious."

"You're welcome, John."

Chapter Twelve

A crescent moon hung in the star-dotted sky. Even though it was just past eight o'clock the town was quiet. Cole and Abigail were the only ones on the street.

"You were a little hard on your aunt, don't you think?"

Pebbles crunched under their footfalls. A lone owl hooted. Abigail fumed. She had not been hard on her aunt.

"She needs to stop interfering."

"Abby, your aunt loves you very much."

"I know. Maybe that's part of the problem, she loves too much."

Frowning at her, Cole said, "You don't really believe that."

She didn't think it possible to ever love someone too much, but having had only one sour relationship, Abigail only had her family to compare love to. As much as she dearly loved her family, she'd sense enough not to cross the line and try to run their lives.

"You know something, Cole? I don't want to discuss this anymore."

"All right, let's just enjoy our evening stroll." He surprised her by linking his arm through hers.

Hesitating, she reluctantly took her arm from his. "This isn't right." Out of the corner of her eye she saw Cole's eyebrow quirk. Sighing, Abigail explained, "We're not some young couple out for a romantic stroll. I'm the Sheriff and you're my prisoner."

Leaning in towards her, he said, "True enough. I thought you might need some help walking over the rough spots. No harm in being a gentleman, is there, Sheriff?"

She met his dark gaze, and seeing the twinkle in his eyes, realized he was teasing her. "No." Smiling she re-linked their arms.

Patting her hand, he said, "Much better. You're doing a fine job as Sheriff."

"Do you think so? I mean I haven't had any experience. You already know that, though." She was nervous.

"It's clear your neighbors like you and feel safe

with you doing the job. You underestimate yourself, Abby. From what I've seen, you are making this job yours."

Thinking about what Cole said, she realized he'd been the only person to tell her she was doing a good job.

"Thank you for being so nice to me."

"You're welcome."

"Now, tell me how you know Wanda McCurdy."

"It's as I mentioned at your aunt's. I met her in Albany. She was a saloon girl, why the curiosity?"

"Something about her doesn't fit. The expensive clothing she wears certainly doesn't go along with her background as a serving girl."

"I noticed her clothing and jewelry too."

They walked along in silence, past the lumber yard and the mercantile before Abigail spoke again. "I have a plan and I need your help to carry it out."

Pulling her to a stop, Cole looked down at her with a raised eyebrow. "What sort of plan?"

"I'm not going to ask you to rob a bank, if that's what you're thinking," she replied, trying to keep the mood light.

"I didn't expect a law-abiding citizen such as yourself to suggest such a thing you know, considering you're the Sheriff and all."

She grinned back at him, continuing with her plan, "There's something suspect about the woman. More than just her appearance, I think." Sucking her lower lip between her teeth, Abigail inhaled, wishing this wasn't so hard. She'd seen how the woman acted around Cole and wasn't sure she wanted to be the one to bring them closer together.

Blowing out the breath she'd been holding, she said, "I need you to get close to her. Find out what she's been doing since she left you in Albany. Find out how it is that she can afford such expensive finery."

"You're kidding, right?"

"No, Cole, I'm perfectly serious about this. If you want to prove your innocence then you're going to have to help me get to the bottom of the jewelry store robbery."

Seeing he needed more convincing, she added, "She seems to have taken a liking to you. Trust my woman's intuition on this; it'll be easier for you to get the answers than it would be for me to."

The more she thought about their situation the more sense her idea made. If she wanted to prove this man's innocence then he was going to have to agree to the plan.

Somewhere over the course of the evening, Abigail decided that she really did believe in his innocence.

"Seeing how Miss McCurdy already has her sights set on me, I guess it won't be too much trouble to help you out."

Continuing their walk, it was hard for her to believe she'd actually asked this man to be a part of such a deception and, furthermore, that he'd agreed to do as she'd asked.

Opening her mouth, she was going to thank him; however, the words were abruptly cut off by the sudden appearance of Wanda McCurdy.

"Fancy running into the two of you!" Wanda said, launching herself at Cole. "Look at you."

Abigail suspected the woman had been lying in wait for them. Her mouth dropped open when Wanda ran her hands over Cole's freshly shaven face, and white hot fury shot through her when he did nothing to stop her.

"I know, quite a difference. Wait until we get where there's some light, you'll see I cut my hair too."

Wanda leaned into him, saying in a breathy voice, "I can't wait."

Cole gave the woman one of those slow, lanquid smiles, showing all of his white teeth. Wanda McCurdy fairly swooned at the sight. Abigail wished they were closer to the rain barrel. A little splash of cold water tossed in their faces would help cool the situation and she'd get a lot of satisfaction being the one to do it.

While it had been her idea to make Wanda think Cole was attracted to her, she didn't expect the sight of them together to bother her this much. Forcing herself to play along, she ordered, "It will have to wait until the morning. Mr. Stanton is due back in his jail cell."

She nodded, curtly, at the flaming redhead and, grabbing hold of Cole's sleeve, pulled him down the street to the sheriff's office. Once inside she gladly opened the cell door and shoved him in.

An entire week had passed and, for all intents and purposes, it appeared barely a civil word had been exchanged between Abigail and Cole. Surprise being the small town that it was, the gossips that gathered in Mr. Jules' store and the men who shared a drink at the end of the day thought they knew all about the sheriff and her prisoner not being on speaking terms.

While for the most part, the townsfolk were figuring that this too would pass, Miss Margaret Monroe Sinclair and her niece, Lydia, weren't so sure. They were sitting on the veranda overlooking the town. From their perch the women could see just about the entire town.

Sipping at the tart lemonade, Lydia shook her head in dismay. "I've never seen Abigail so upset and I know I've never seen her this angry before." She paused, taking another sip. "Come to think of it, I can't recall ever seeing her in such a tizzy."

"I'm sure when Edwin left her she was in a tizzy," Margaret said.

"That was different. I don't think she was attracted to Edwin. Leastwise not in the way she's attracted to Mr. Stanton."

Margaret mulled the statement over, sipping out of the tall glass. The sound of hammers banging nails into the roof of the new schoolhouse echoed in the small valley. Margaret smiled. Her plan was moving along quite nicely, she thought. The school would be finished by fall, and she had two of her precious nieces by her side. Maggie would be along anytime now.

The problem was Abigail. Margaret wondered when her niece had become so stubborn? She'd never been that way before. A little backbone was one thing, but not listening to reason was quite another. And right now Abigail wasn't listening to anyone.

"There are such sparks between them when they are together," Lydia mused.

"I have to agree. Why, the other night, when they entered the dining room, arm in arm, I thought they looked so lovely."

Lydia swatted at a big yellow bumblebee that buzzed in front of her face. "They did. This is all Wanda McCurdy's fault. Everything was going along fine until she showed up in town."

"Yes, I have to agree. Miss McCurdy definitely has designs on Mr. Stanton."

"And Abigail thinks she's no match for the ghastly woman," Lydia said, slowly.

They fell silent, each lost in her own thoughts. Finally, Margaret said, "Well, she's wrong. Abigail is a beautiful young, intelligent woman with a lot to offer the right man."

Their voices one, Lydia and Margaret spoke, "And Cole Stanton is the right man."

"How are we going to get those two together?" Margaret asked.

"They ought to be locked up in the same jail cell," Lydia joked.

"Why, Lydia Louise Monroe, what a brilliant idea! I always knew you were the devious one. This is perfect."

Putting their heads together they whispered secret plans back and forth for a few hurried minutes. Smiling, they clinked their glasses together, toasting their scheme.

Chapter Thirteen

From where he stood in Judson's lumber yard, Cole was able to see the comings and goings of one stubborn female sheriff. Near as he could tell, she was still worked up over Wanda's brash antics. Lord help him, but he didn't like hurting anyone, least of all Abigail, but getting close to Wanda had been *her* idea. He was only obliging her wishes.

It was the only way to prove his innocence, and she shouldn't be so upset by how well things were going.

Wanda McCurdy held his future in her hands. It looked like the said future was going to be shorter than he'd hoped because rumor had it that the circuit judge was slowly making his way to Surprise. In fact, Cole had been informed by Mr. Wagner just this morning that the judge was presiding over court just thirty miles north of Catskill.

Time was running out. And that was why, when Wanda had sashayed herself over here with a picnic basket brimming with food, he acted thrilled to see her. Cole wanted his freedom back. Wanda had set him up, he was certain of it, and with the sheriff on his side it would be easier to prove.

Of course life being the way it was when women were involved, it didn't help any that since their moonlit stroll, he'd been thinking about the sheriff in a rather unlawful way. Looking forward to the end of the day when she'd walk him back to the jail, thinking about goodnight kisses and how her soft skin would feel beneath his fingertips.

He'd worked so hard for so long at not putting down roots and now he wasn't sure that he'd be able to turn his back on this town as easily as he had all the others. Cole was falling in love with Abigail Monroe and there was only one thing he could do to stop it; leave town.

He had to get Wanda to admit to the robbery before it was too late, before there was no turning back.

"Cole, are you coming?" Wanda batted her long brown eyelashes at him. "I thought we could eat over by the big oak tree."

It didn't escape his notice that this particular spot was in plain view. Of course they'd sat under this tree a time or two before, but that was when he'd been teasing Abigail. Putting down his hammer, he joined Wanda. Taking the heavy wicker basket from her, he followed her to the bench.

Smoothing down the folds of her voluminous red skirts, she seated herself on the bench, saying, "My, my. What a lovely day for a picnic."

"Yes, ma'am, it sure is." Cole struggled to be as polite as could be. He was going to get the truth out of her one way or the other starting today.

"You know, Cole, I still can't get used to seeing you without your beard and long hair." Reaching into the basket she took out a waxpaper-wrapped sandwich. Patting the space next to her on the bench, she bade him to sit next to her.

He did and, unwrapping the sandwich, found he'd lost his appetite. Abigail was walking out of the mercantile with some papers in her hand. Glancing up and down both sides of the street, her gaze swung to them. Cole felt his mouth go dry. *Shoot.* He felt like a cad sitting here with Wanda.

She nodded her approval. Though, even from this distance he could tell by the set of her shoulders her feelings were hurt.

"Cole? Is something wrong?"

Forcing his attention back to the woman seated next to him, Cole shook his head. It was time to get down to business. The sunlight glinted off Wanda's earrings. Cole darn near choked on his sandwich. If this woman was the jewel thief, she was as bold as brass wearing the stolen goods out in public.

"Lovely earrings. Where did you get them from?"

Reaching up she toyed with the sapphires. "Oh these silly things, they're just some costume pieces that my mother left me." She laughed a shaky nervous sound.

Yeah and pigs could fly. He'd have to find out from Abigail the exact description of the pieces stolen. If she ever started speaking to him again, he'd ask her.

"How much longer before the judge arrives?"

"I heard he's presiding in court about thirty miles from here. Should be any day now, I imagine." Cole wanted her confession in such a bad way, that he leaned over and took her hand in his. "I'm afraid our time together is coming to an end."

Leaning in close to him she said, oh so softly, "It doesn't have to be that way. You could escape and go away with me."

Now there was a plan. He cupped her face in his hands, rubbing his thumbs along the smooth surface of the gemstones in her earrings. These were definitely the real thing.

Her big blue eyes searched his face. "You look so different, so handsome. You know you don't resemble the Wanted poster one single bit now."

He froze. When had she seen the Wanted poster? As far as he knew Abigail had kept it in her desk drawer since arresting him. Nuzzling his nose alongside her ear, he went in for the kill. "Where did you see the poster?"

Was it his imagination or did Miss McCurdy just tense up? Pulling away from her, he studied her face. She was looking at a spot just above his left shoulder; still he didn't mistake the flicker of hesitation that appeared in her eyes. The one sure sign she knew she'd messed up her story.

"I saw it hanging on the board outside of the Sheriff's office." Running her hand down his sleeve, she asked, "Must we spoil our day with such disturbing talk. The judge will be here soon and your innocence will be proven. Then we can go away together."

Wanda was living in a dream world if she thought for one minute that he'd be going away with her. Given the option, he'd rather stay incarcerated.

"We'll have to see about that."

Cole stood, packing up the remains of their lunch. "I have to get back to work, Wanda. Thanks for the sandwiches."

Before he could escape, she stood on tiptoe and kissed him on the cheek. "There's more where that came from."

"I'll keep that in mind." Turning around he headed back to the lumber yard. He'd still a full afternoon of work to be done. Alexander wanted him to finish cutting the floor planking for the schoolhouse. Cole hadn't felt this satisfied with a day's work in a very long time. He realized how much he'd missed working with his hands.

He hadn't gone halfway across the yard when he got the feeling he was being watched. Slowly he looked back over his shoulder and there in the doorway of the Sheriff's office with her arms folded across her chest, stood Abigail.

Even from this distance he could see that she looked angrier than a bunch of bees knocked out of their hive. He braced his feet apart and put his hands on his hips, wondering if she were just putting on a show for the busybodies? She was striding towards him at full steam, her anger looking fairly convincing to him.

By the time Abigail reached him, the smooth skin across her cheekbones had reddened and she was slightly out of breath. Looking at her, it finally struck him that she wasn't playacting, Sheriff Abigail Monroe was about ready to pop!

"It's time to go back to jail."

"I haven't finished cutting the wood for today's order."

"You can finish it tomorrow. Right now I'm taking you back to jail." With little fanfare, she grabbed his arm and led him back across the street.

By the time they reached the building it was clear

that her anger wasn't going away anytime soon. He allowed her to take him inside without uttering a word of protest or explanation.

They were both surprised to find Lydia there.

"Lydia, what on earth are you doing inside the jail cell?" Abigail demanded to know.

"I scared a chipmunk in here by mistake. The little scamp ran right under my skirts the minute I opened your door. Then it ran right past me into this cell." Her green eyes widened in innocence. "I can't seem to get the creature to come out from behind the bunk."

Cole moved past Abigail. "Let me see if I can get him."

Abigail hurried along behind him, standing just inside the cell while Cole knelt on the floor, peering under the bunk.

"I don't see anything."

"He ran along the back. Abigail, you might have to look on the other end."

While the two of them were hunkered down on the floor looking for Lydia's chipmunk, she slowly backed out of the cell.

Chapter Fourteen

Neither Cole nor Abigail knew what hit them, until the steel-barred door clanked closed behind them.

Abigail sprang to her feet, shouting at her cousin, "Lydia Louise Monroe, you let me out of here right this instant!"

Wrapping her hands around the steel bars, she pulled back and forth, trying to release the lock on the door.

"Let me out!"

Lydia backed towards the front door. "I can't. You have to stay in there until you and Mr. Stanton settle your differences."

"We don't have any differences!" Abigail shouted back.

"Abigail, this is for your own good," Lydia said in soothing tones. "There's a box in the corner with some dinner in it."

"Lydia!" Abigail yelled. Lydia pulled the shades down on all the windows, tacked a DO NOT DISTURB sign to the front door, waved good-bye and gently closed the door behind her.

Abigail wanted to throttle her dear, sweet cousin and her aunt, who more than likely had played a part in this. "She ambushed us," Abigail said in dismay. "Lydia was laying in wait for us!"

Resting her chin on a cold bar, she looked longingly out into her office at the key ring hanging tauntingly by the front door. There was no way to reach them. Sighing, Abigail resigned herself to the fact that she was stuck in here until some kind soul came by to let them out.

Behind her, the bunk creaked under Cole's weight as he sat down. He was definitely taking this better than she was. Slowly she turned around to face him. Leaning against the cell door, she carefully folded her arms across her chest.

"Looks to me like our little plan backfired. Got any bright ideas on how to get us out of here, Sheriff?"

"Don't you go blaming me for this, Cole Stanton! I had no way of knowing what Lydia was up to."

"It looks to me like we're going to have a long time to think about that, aren't we?"

Angry, Abigail didn't see the point in answering him. Though, it did warm her heart just a bit to see that Cole appeared to be just as unhappy as she was about their situation. He looked rather glum sitting there with his elbows on his knees and his chin resting in his hands. Nibbling on her lower lip, she wondered how long they would be able to remain silent.

The clock on the wall on the right side of her desk ticked away the seconds, which turned into minutes, which ever so slowly turned into half an hour. In the space of that time neither of them had moved very far. She'd shifted from her right foot to the left, and Cole had taken his head out of his hands which now dangled listlessly between his legs.

Their eyes met.

"Are you attracted to Wanda McCurdy?"

"Do you think I'm guilty of robbery?"

Simultaneously they responded, "Is that what you think?"

She almost smiled then, but the time had come to face their problems head on. The first of which was the question of his guilt or innocence. She wasn't ready to face what her jealous reaction to Wanda McCurdy was all about.

"Honestly, Cole. I don't know whether or not you're guilty. All I know is until you shaved your beard off you fit the description on the Wanted poster. And the timing for the crime may have fit a time when you were passing through Albany."

She longed to tell him that deep down in her heart, she knew he wasn't capable of such an act. Something held her back. Perhaps it was a cautionary reaction. She'd mistakenly given her heart to Edwin and look where that had gotten her. There was no way she'd make the same blunder twice.

Tired of standing, she sat down at the opposite end of the bunk. The clock on the wall chimed six times. Silently Abigail counted the hours until daylight, twelve. Twelve long hours with nowhere to go and no one to talk to except a man she wholeheartedly wanted to loathe, and yet couldn't bring herself to do so.

Abigail's stomach began to growl with hunger pangs. Eyeing the box that Lydia had referred to, she wondered what delicious food Anna had prepared for a jailhouse dinner?

"Are you hungry? Because Lydia left us some food if you are." Shifting her weight on the bunk, Abigail leaned over and opened the lid to the box. Wonderful, delectable scents filled the air.

Was that fried chicken she was smelling, and apple pie? A part of her was delighted with the find, but a bigger part of her was still angry with her family for locking her in here with Cole. She was also angry with herself. She'd been so preoccupied doing her job that she hadn't seen this coming.

Peering around her, Cole said, "Looks to me like they thought of everything."

"Didn't they, though," Abigail murmured. She could feel Cole's warm breath against the back of her neck.

Handing him a plate, she proceeded to fill it with chicken, biscuits, pickled beans and a slice of apple pie. After doing the same for herself, she gingerly set the plate on her lap. Trying not to notice his close proximity, Abigail bit into a piece of chicken.

They ate in silence and when they were finished Cole reached out to take her plate. Their hands brushed, sending a shock of delight down her arm. Determined not to look him directly in the eyes, Abigail concentrated on staring at a spot just to the right of his head.

She was quiet as he cleaned up, putting the plates back into the box. Abigail studied him. His brow was furrowed in concentration. Cole's shoulders were broad and his hands callused from working at the lumber yard. Blinking, she realized that he was looking at her. His gaze darkened in intensity as his face softened.

"I'm not interested in Wanda McCurdy." It was a statement, one that brooked no argument.

Smoothing the folds on her skirt, she replied, "It sure looks to me and the rest of the town, like you are interested."

"Well I'm not." He stood with his back resting

against the wall, he arms folded across his massive chest and his feet crossed at the ankles of his long muscular legs.

"Then why do you spend so much time with her?"

"You've got to be joking? Remember how you asked me to *pretend* to be interested in her?"

"You certainly didn't have to be so convincing about it!"

"You're jealous!" He started to laugh. "You are really jealous of Wanda McCurdy. Well, I'll be . . ."

She snorted. "I am not jealous."

It was his turn to snort.

"Look, Abby, I didn't rob the jewelry store."

"I know you didn't. But the fact still remains that the description on the poster is a match to you. There's no denying it, Cole."

He was looking at her as if he could see right through her. One minute he wanted her to think like a Sheriff, cold and calculating, while the next minute he was asking her to think like a woman. She'd pushed her feelings for him aside so many times over the past weeks that it was difficult to admit to herself and to him how she really felt.

Pushing himself away from the wall, he sat next to her. "Look, Wanda knows something about that robbery. Do you have any descriptions of the pieces that were stolen?"

She shook her head. "I don't remember seeing

anything like that. But, it doesn't mean that we can't find out. I could always send a telegram to the authorities in Albany asking for the description."

"That may not be necessary. Let me ask you something else—did you ever hang the Wanted poster outside on the notice board?"

"No. As soon as I realized you fit the description, I tucked it away in the desk drawer where I keep most of the older notices."

He pondered her answer for a few minutes and said, "Wanda said she saw the poster hanging outside the office. She mentioned that with my beard gone I no longer looked like the description."

"If she hasn't ever seen the Wanted poster, then how could she possibly know what the description said? Unless . . ."

He smiled, and finished her sentence. "Unless she was the one who gave my description to the authorities in Albany."

Frowning, Abigail wondered allowed, "What if she saw the poster someplace else, like on the train or in a newspaper?"

"I don't think so. Wanda specifically said that she saw the poster hanging outside your office."

"Let's say that she was involved in the robbery, where is the jewelry?"

"I think she has some of it on her. Those sapphire earrings she had on the other day were real."

Abigail stood and began pacing the cell thinking

about what Cole had just told her. If all of this were true then she had the wrong man behind bars. Nibbling on her lower lip, she studied the tips of her shoes. Was it possible that he'd been telling the truth all along and she'd been too stubborn to investigate further?

Feeling slightly ashamed, Abigail raised her eyes and, looking at Cole, said, "I'm sorry for not believing you before this all happened."

He seemed surprised at her apology and, rising from the bunk, he stood before her. "You were just doing your job."

"Yes and a fine job I made of it. I didn't even look any further than you for a suspect, even when you told me you didn't do it. Maybe this town needs a new sheriff, one who will do the job right."

"This town doesn't want another sheriff, they want you. Abigail, you're doing a good job here. I told you so the other night and I meant it."

Abigail smiled. "Thank you."

Placing his hand under her chin, he tipped her head back. "I'm going to kiss you."

"Oh!"

Lowering his head, Cole placed his lips on hers. At first she didn't respond, and then slowly she moved her lips against his. They felt warm and moist upon hers. Her heartbeat quickened as Cole deepened the kiss. Slowly he broke away and gathered her in his arms.

"I've been wanting to do that for the longest time," he murmured against her ear.

Uncertainty flooded through her. How could she let this man kiss her? After all, she didn't even know anything about him. Weeks had passed since they first met and still, he hadn't told her who he was or where he'd grown up. Did he have sisters and brothers, she wondered? If she was going to give her heart to this man, then she needed to know who he was.

Without taking her head off his shoulder, Abigail said, "Tell me who you are, Cole."

Chapter Fifteen

Cole blew out the breath he'd been holding. He shouldn't have given in to the impulse to kiss her. Now she was in his arms, feeling as if she'd always belonged there. Cole sighed. There was so much to tell and he didn't know what to say. He wasn't even certain that he wanted to tell anyone about his past; even the woman he was falling in love with.

"Cole?"

He tried to muster up a smile for her, but the only thing he managed was a frown. "I hardly know where to begin."

"Try the beginning. Tell me where you lived as a little boy."

He wanted to capture the look of enthusiasm and innocence that appeared on Abigail's face and keep it with him forever. Because, even now all these years later, he still felt raw, unhealed, his pain like an open wound that refused to close up.

Cole would keep his explanation as simple as possible. "I had a younger sister. My mother and father had settled along the banks of the upper Hudson River. We had a log cabin just big enough for my family."

Oh God! He couldn't do this, even for Abigail, he couldn't go back to that place in his life that bore nothing but pain and agony for him. Releasing her, he turned and scrubbed his hands over his face trying to erase any look of pain.

Forcing his hands not to shake, he lit the lantern hanging on the wall near the bunk. The flame sputtered and then took. He set the lantern on the table.

"What is your sister's name?"

"Her name was Beth."

"Was? Did something happen to her?" She took a step towards him and laid her hand upon his arm.

This was agony for him and yet seeing the compassion shining in Abigail's eyes, he knew that he had to tell her everything. "She died. A very long time ago, my parents and Beth died from influenza."

"Oh Cole, I'm so terribly sorry. I shouldn't have gone on and on about your family. Please, forgive me."

Leaning against the cold steel bars of their prison, he said, gruffly, "There's nothing to forgive. It's been a long time since I've spoken about what happened."

The flame from the lantern flickered as evening shadows spread over the room. It was quiet. Abigail was standing very near to him and he could hear her shallow breathing. He could almost sense what she was thinking and wished she'd leave him alone.

"The nightmares, they were about your family weren't they?" She spoke softly as if fearing any loudness would set him off.

He nodded. "They started soon after I buried them in our apple orchard. Little Beth loved apples. Applesauce, mama's apple pie, apples cut into small chunks. She could never get enough of them."

Abigail smiled at him and said in soothing tones, "What a wonderful memory."

"She was so young, still a baby." He felt as if his heart was splitting open.

"I can tell that you loved your family very much."

He rested his head against the bars feeling exhausted and heartbroken all over again. Cole knew that he'd been better off not getting attached to anyone or anything. He vowed a long time ago never to open his heart, never to share his life with anyone. How did Abigail work her way into his life? When had he become so attached to this town?

Feelings of frustration, rage, sadness and loneliness rolled through him at the same time. Abigail had backed away from him and was standing near the edge of the bunk. It was as if she felt his pain and knew that even she couldn't reach through the suffering and pull him out whole again.

"I can see that you're not ready, even after all these years, to face the memories—good or bad. I'm going to tell you something Cole, and all I'm asking is that you listen carefully to what I have to say before responding."

She sat on the end of the bed and crossed her legs. "I can't profess to understand how horrible the death of your family was, but looking at you right now, I can see it still tearing away at your soul. I know that we got off to a very rocky start and that you don't think Surprise holds any kind of a life for you, but if you give the town a chance you may see that it just might."

He couldn't speak. Raw emotions threatened to choke him, so he concentrated on her words.

"Cole, it's time for you to start to live again, to trust that life holds more happiness for you. You're not going to defile their memory if you start to feel alive again. I believe your family would want you to be happy. Don't you believe that, too, Cole?"

He didn't know what to believe in anymore. Cole wanted to believe in Abigail Monroe, he wanted to let her into his heart in the most desperate way. There was still so much he didn't know about her.

"Tell me, Abby, why did you leave your fiance at the altar?"

Surprised by his question, she jumped up from the bed and walked over to him. "I did not leave Edwin at the altar. He left me."

Quirking an eyebrow, he looked at her and caught a glimpse of the old pain she'd kept carefully hidden. So she'd had her heart broken too, but in a different way. He imagined it hurt all the same.

"That must have been very difficult for you."

"At first, yes it was. Then I realized I didn't love Edwin and going our separate ways was for the best."

He pondered her insight for a moment and then said, "You came to Surprise for a new start."

"I suppose I did. Aunt Margaret helped me make the decision to come here."

He snorted at her words. "Miss Margaret helps a lot of people with their lives doesn't she?"

Shrugging her shoulders, she replied, "She enjoys helping others. It's her calling."

Meddling was more like what she did, but Cole wasn't going to argue the point with Abigail, not when they were so close to each other.

The clock struck nine times. "Time is just flying by," Cole muttered.

"Let's talk about your work release program. Tell me how you find working with Alexander Judson?"

"I enjoy working with my hands. Before I came here I had a small construction company of my own."

"Why did you leave your company?"

"I was beginning to feel closed in." Truth be told he'd been feeling at home and that had scared him. All he could remember was how it felt to lose everything one holds dear. And he ran.

"I'm sorry."

Looking into the depths of her blue-green eyes he saw that she was sorry, but more than that, he saw her compassion.

Leaning down, he touched his lips lightly to her forehead. He couldn't help himself. Cole wanted to kiss those lips again.

Reaching out to him, Abigail cupped his face in her hands and brought her lips to his. For several minutes Cole lost himself in the feeling of her kisses. Then gently he extricated himself from her grasp. "We need to stop."

"Why? Am I doing it wrong?"

"Oh, no, you are doing everything right and that is why we're going to stop kissing right this minute. You may sit on one end of the bunk and I'll sit on the other."

Satisfied when he'd put some distance between them, Cole settled into his end of the bunk. He rested his head against the brick wall thinking about the feelings that Abigail brought out in him. He found, along with his undeniable attraction to her, came a need to want to protect her.

He couldn't help thinking about her former fiance—Edwin was a fool. Abigail still hadn't told him why Edwin left her.

"Why didn't Edwin marry you?"

She lifted her head and looked across the bunk at him. Her gaze was clear and steady, but Cole didn't miss the look of pain that crossed once more through her beautiful blue-green eyes.

Softly she answered, "I wasn't pretty enough for him."

Cole's eyebrows shot skyward. "What?" he fairly bellowed.

"He wanted someone blonder and well you know . . . shapelier." With a quick shrug of her shoulders she added, "I didn't fit his image of what he wanted his wife to be."

"It sounds to me like he wanted someone shallow, a woman who he could parade around on his arm."

"I suppose so."

Daring to move inches closer to Abigail, Cole said with affirmation, "Look at me, Abby." When finally she did, he smiled. "This Edwin, what's his last name?"

"Quinn."

"Edwin Quinn is a fool to have let you go. You're pretty, compassionate, intelligent, and witty."

Frowning as if she didn't believe a word he'd just spoken, Abigail said, "You sound like you're writing an advertisement for the newspaper."

Grinning at her, Cole reached out and gently ran his hand along the smooth skin of her cheek. "Well, I'm not. I'm trying to tell you that I think you're wonderful."

Her eyes glistened. He caught the first tear as it slid from her eye.

"No man has ever said anything like what you just said to me. Thank you."

"You're welcome."

Sniffing, she pulled a white handkerchief from her pocket, gently wiped her eyes and blew her nose. Putting the kerchief back in her pocket, she settled against his shoulder. "I think you're wonderful too." Putting her hand over her mouth, Abigail stifled a yawn.

"It's getting late, Sheriff, we should try to get some sleep."

"Yes, it appears that Lydia isn't coming back until morning."

Reaching for the blanket, Abigail added, "Tomorrow we'll get this whole mess settled and then we'll deal with what's going on between us."

Slanting her a look, he asked, "There's something between us?"

"I'm afraid so." Snuggling under the blanket, Abigail closed her eyes.

For the longest time, Cole just watched her sleep. Noting the way her long silky eyelashes rested against her skin, and liking the way her mouth, even in sleep, was curved ever so gently into the smallest of smiles. Only when she was completely asleep did he settle back against the hard wall.

Sighing, he waited for sleep to come and, when it did, he dreamed that he was sitting under the apple tree in the backyard where he grew up. Beth was dancing around him, her little feet gently turning down the blades of grass. She was holding a brilliant red apple and the sunlight glinted off her downy hair.

He smiled as he heard Beth's bubbly laughter. Suddenly Cole felt warm and alive, he felt Beth's small hand as she placed the apple inside of his. Beside him in the bunk, Abigail shifted her position, curling up next to him with her head in his lap. He awoke with a start, taking a minute to remember where he was.

Stroking a hand over Abigail's hair, he smiled; this was the first time he'd ever had a good dream about his family. He owed that to Abigail. His heart swelled as some of the old pain left his soul.

Chapter Sixteen

The train's shrill whistle woke her. Abigail sat up with a start. Cole was already awake and standing with his back to her, looking out at the office.

"Lydia isn't here?"

"Not yet," he said.

Pushing the blanket aside, she got up, straightening out her skirt and hair. What a mess she must be. "What time is it?"

"A quarter past seven."

"The train is early."

Turning, he looked at her. Abigail thought she had to be mistaken, but she wasn't. Cole was actually smiling at her. She also noticed that he looked decidedly more relaxed than she'd ever seen him before. Gone was the grim look which had always seemed to shadow his eyes, and even his smile appeared more genuine.

Even though she was dying to know what had brought about this change in him, it would have to wait. Right now they had to get out of there and find Wanda McCurdy before she figured out they were on to her.

"Don't you have a hidden key or something we can use to open this door?" Cole asked as he shook the bars.

"I don't have another key. Sadly the only ones I have are hanging over there on the wall." She nodded in the direction of the front door, where the keys still hung taunting them both.

Turning around in a slow circle, Abigail began looking about the cell, trying to see if there wasn't something they could use to unlatch the lock. She began to rummage through the box that their dinner had been in and yelled when something sharp bit into her hand.

"Ouch." Lifting her hand out of the box, she examined the small drops of blood coming from the tip of her finger. "I didn't see anything sharp in here last night."

"Are you all right?" Cole took her hand in his and looked at the small puncture wound. He kissed the tip of each finger, and said, "To make them heal faster."

Taking her hand from his, Abigail reached gingerly into the box and pulled out a small sandwich knife. It had been there all along, except not where you'd notice it, unless a person had been looking for it.

"Lydia!" Abigail hissed. Her cousin was quite the sneak, giving them a way out, without telling them ahead of time.

Handing the knife to Cole, she said, "Here, you break us out."

After a few minutes of jiggling the knife in the lock, the door sprung open and they were freed.

By eight o'clock in the morning the town was bustling with activity. The two freight cars on the train were being unloaded while farmers and merchants loaded their wagons with the goods. Lydia hurried along to the jail, figuring that by now Abigail and Mr. Stanton were more than ready to be set free.

Pausing, she lifted the cloth napkin off the top of the basket she carried and inhaled the sweet scent of the cinnamon rolls she'd helped Anne bake earlier that morning. *My, what a wonderful day it was*, she thought. Hopefully, her cousin and Mr. Stanton had reconciled their differences. If not, she didn't know what she would have to do next.

"Lydia! Lydia Louise, is it really you!"

Turning at the sound of the familiar voice, Lydia could hardly believe her eyes. "Oh my gosh, Maggie!" Dropping the basket in front of the sheriff's office she ran across the street to embrace her cousin.

"Maggie! Oh, Maggie I'm so glad you're here. You're not going to believe what's been going on in Surprise."

"From the looks of things I'd say quite a bit. When did this town become so popular?"

Ushering her back across the street, Lydia answered, "It's been changing over the past couple of months. I've only been here for three weeks and already the new schoolhouse has gone up."

Stopping in front of the sheriff's office, Lydia stooped to pick up the basket. Carefully she opened the door and peered inside, listening for any disgruntled sounds. She imagined that the two lovebirds would be hungry and just a bit cranky after being locked up all night.

There was no sound, and when she opened the door the rest of the way she saw the reason why. No one was here. The cell door was opened. Setting the basket on the desk, she walked over to look inside the cell. The blankets on the bunk were rumpled and looked as if they'd been slept on.

Since she hadn't seen them at home or on her way here, Lydia wondered where they'd gone. A large shadow filled the doorway of the office. Slowly, Lydia turned around and found herself staring at a stout man.

"May I help you, sir?" Lydia gulped, and Maggie moved closer to her cousin as if she might be able to protect her.

"I'm looking for a prisoner by the name of Cole Stanton and Sheriff Abigail Monroe." Looking up from the sheet of paper he held in his pudgy hand, he asked, "Is your sheriff a woman?"

Both women nodded.

Peering around their shoulders he said, "Looks to me like they're not here. Do you happen to know where they are?"

Both women shook their heads.

"Come on. I know where Wanda is staying," Abigail said, as they walked rapidly along the back of the buildings. The first place they'd gone to was the telegraph office, where Abigail had sent an inquiry to the authorities in Albany asking for a description of the stolen goods.

Two strides ahead of her, Cole replied, "At the boardinghouse."

"Let's hope she's still there."

By the time they got to Mrs. Bartholomew's house the morning sun was warming up the day, drying the dew on the front lawn. Abigail proceeded up the steps with Cole behind her. Wasting no time, she rapped her knuckles against the front door. Within minutes Mrs. Bartholomew answered the door.

"Morning, Sheriff Abigail." She nodded politely at Cole. "Mr. Stanton." Closing the door behind her, she joined them on the porch. "I've got a few boarders who aren't early risers. We'll just talk out here so as not to disturb them."

"Would Wanda McCurdy be one of those late risers?" Abigail asked.

"Why yes, she is. How did you know?"

"A lucky guess." Abigail figured that someone as obviously vain as Miss McCurdy would be spending as much time as she could getting the required amount of beauty rest.

Beside her Cole impatiently shifted his weight from one foot to the other. Abigail was well aware of the importance of talking to Wanda.

"Do you think we might have a word with Miss McCurdy?" Cole asked before Abigail could even form the words.

Slanting him a look to remind that she was in charge, she turned and smiled at Mrs. Bartholomew. "If you don't mind, we really need to speak to Miss. McCurdy."

"Normally I don't like to disturb my boarders. You know I run a good business and part of that is not bothering people when they are sleeping."

Obviously they'd insulted her. Laying a hand on her arm, Abigail said, "I know that you're the best landlady in Surprise. We wouldn't ask to speak to Miss McCurdy unless it was important."

Looking from Cole to Abigail, Mrs. Bartholomew smiled. "I guess I could see if she's awake. You two make yourself comfortable on those rockers and I'll be right back."

Abigail didn't feel much like relaxing. She wanted this to be over with so she could get on with her life. But more important, so Cole could get on with his. After last night's revelations she wasn't certain what was going to happen with their relationship. She knew that if and when he was a free man, only then would they be able to find out what their future held.

Five minutes later a flushed and out-of-breath landlady burst onto the front porch. "She's gone! That woman up and left in the middle of the night without so much as a thank you, and she skipped out on paying her bill!"

Abigail and Cole were off the porch at the same time. They could hear the train rolling out of town. Stopping, they looked at each other and then took off running through town.

"We need to catch that train!" Abigail shouted.

By the time they reached the platform the train was making its way over the rise. "Come on. I know where Mr. Jules keeps his horse and buggy."

Leading the way to the stable, Abigail showed Cole where the tack was and helped him hitch up the horse. By the time they left the stable, a small crowd had gathered.

"Hey, Sheriff, where are you off to in such a hurry?"

"She's got that criminal with her," yelled another person.

Slapping the reins against the horse's backside, Cole got them moving at a rapid pace. As they galloped out of town with the buggy barely riding on four wheels, Abigail hung onto the side of the seat for dear life.

They were out of hearing distance like a shot. Neither of them heard when Mr. Jules jumped to the conclusion that Cole must be using the sheriff as a hostage so he could make a clean getaway. So while they left a trail of dust in their wake, the townsfolk were rounding up a posse.

"Hurry, Cole. We can't let her get away!" Abigail balanced herself in the seat while keeping a hand on her head to keep her hat from sailing off.

"There's the caboose." Cole urged the horse onward.

Before he could stop her, Abigail positioned herself on the edge of the seat, preparing to jump onto the steps of the caboose. For her it was reminiscent of the time she'd captured Cole leaving on this very train. At least now she was going to get the real criminal.

"Pull up closer," she ordered.

Without questioning her wisdom or her sanity,

Cole pulled alongside the car. On the silent count of three, Abigail, with her skirts flying around her, launched herself onto the steps. Her footing firm, she reached into her pocket, drew her gun, and entered the caboose. From there she made her way through two passenger cars before finding the woman she was looking for.

It wasn't difficult to find her because she was wearing a ridiculous hat with the fake bird and bright orange dried flowers. The color clashed with her flaming red hair.

Quietly, Abigail made her way down the aisle while Wanda was oblivious to the activity going on around her. Noticing the vacant seat on the window side of Wanda's, Abigail asked, "Is this seat taken?"

The welcoming smile on Wanda's face faded as soon as she saw who asked the question. "Sheriff Abigail!"

Abigail thought she heard a gurgling sound coming from the woman but wasn't certain until she saw the skin on Wanda's face turning puce. Realizing that the woman was choking, she thumped her hard on the back.

When the coughing finally subsided, Abigail leaned down asking, "Better now?"

Her hand clutching her throat, Wanda nodded mournfully. The train began to slow down as Abigail trained her gun on Wanda.

"You almost got away with it, Miss McCurdy. I must say that framing a drifter like Cole Stanton was brilliant thinking on your part."

Wanda stuttered, "I don't . . . know . . . what you're talking about."

Admiring the sapphire earrings worn by Wanda, Abigail reached out to touch the smooth stones. "I think you know exactly what I'm talking about."

Outside the soot-stained window Abigail watched as Cole drove the carriage up to the front of the train. Wanda noticed him too.

Pointing her finger towards the window, Wanda wailed, "He did it! Cole Stanton robbed that jewelry store in Albany!"

Her hysterical shrieking roused the curiosity of the dozen or so passengers sharing the car, causing them to peer over their seats. Some even stood in the aisle trying to ascertain what all the commotion was about.

Hoping to ward off anymore hysteria, Abigail ordered everyone to sit down. "Miss McCurdy, you know as well as I do that Mr. Stanton did not rob the jewelry store. I believe these earrings are proof of that."

Shaking her head violently, Wanda said, "No, they were a gift from a friend."

With brakes squealing and the cars shifting, the train pulled to a stop.

Taking hold of Wanda's hand, Abigail pulled her

from the seat. "Wanda McCurdy, I'm placing you under arrest for robbery."

"No! No! You can't do this to me." Her hat slid down onto her shoulder and pins fell from her hair. Despite her disheveled appearance, Wanda continued to violently shake her head.

By the time Abigail managed to drag her through the car and out onto the platform, Wanda was crying and clutching her traveling bag to her chest with a death-defying grip.

While the commotion inside the train car had been bad, the chaos that greeted them as they departed the train was even worse.

Chapter Seventeen

Mayhem and mass hysteria seemed to have become the rule of the day. A trail of dust could be seen as far back as Surprise. Wagons and riders on horseback were circling in front of where Abigail stood holding onto Wanda. There was a great deal of shouting going on, none of which could be discerned.

Doing the only thing she could think of, Abigail raised her arm above her head and fired a single shot into the air.

"What is the meaning of this?" Searching the crowd, surrounding Cole, Abigail set her sights on Mr. Jules. "Mr. Jules, perhaps you'd care to explain."

He spent an inordinate amount of time shuffling

his feet in the dirt and then adjusting his clothing. Finally raising his eyes to meet her stare, he said, "We captured the escapee."

She felt her eyes widen.

"See, a bunch of us witnessed Mr. Stanton here taking you as hostage. We saw him making a get-away in my buggy."

She knew when her mouth dropped open, and quickly snapped it shut.

Beside her Wanda spoke up, adding fuel to the crowd's anger. "Look, they've captured the real criminal, now you can let me go."

In any other place and any other town, Abigail would have thought them all completely insane, but these were the citizens of Surprise and nothing here was ever ordinary.

Wanda struggled to break free and in doing so dropped her satchel on the ground. The fall caused the clasp to break open and the contents to spill forth. The sunlight glinted off the sparkly jewelry. Wanda began to shriek about being set up by Cole.

The crowd began to pick up momentum once more, gathering around Cole, upon whom many hands held in place. The look on his face was so funny that Abigail wanted to laugh. His dark eyes were fixed upon her, the look beseeching her to do something. Springing into action, she stepped down from the train.

"Let Mr. Stanton go. He's done nothing wrong.

As a matter of fact as soon as the circuit judge arrives he will be cleared of all charges."

The crowd separated and released Cole. Realizing the ground in front of them was splattered with priceless jewels, they turned their attention to admiring the cache.

"Don't touch the jewelry, these items are evidence of Miss Wanda McCurdy's crime."

"You can't prove that I did this!" Wanda squirmed to break free.

"I'm afraid that she can." John Wagner stepped forth from the crowd waving a piece of paper in his hand. "This just came in to the telegraph office, the descriptions of all the stolen property." Glancing from the paper to the ground, he declared, "Looks to me like we've got a match."

Pushing her hat back up on her head, Wanda raised her chin, straightened her spine and allowed Abigail to lead her to the waiting buggy. Glancing over her shoulder Abigail was relieved to see that the crowd had released Cole. Tipping his hat to her, he waved her along. They rode back to town in Mr. Jules' buggy with a ragtag caravan of townspeople following them. When she finally pulled the buggy to a halt in front of the sheriff's office, Abigail was surprised to find Aunt Margaret sitting out front in her wheelchair.

"Glad to see you made it back in one piece, Sheriff Abigail." Her aunt's voice carried crystal clear over the hubbub of the town returning.

Helping Wanda down, Abigail led her to the doorway, pausing to peck her aunt on the cheek. "I'm glad you felt well enough to come out."

Winking at her, Aunt Margaret replied, "I wouldn't have missed this for the world." Grabbing hold of her sleeve, she stopped Abigail long enough to add, "I'd be careful if I were you, you've got plenty of company in there." She nodded towards the office.

Smiling weakly, Abigail escorted Wanda Mc-Curdy in through the open door. The first person she noticed was Lydia. Dear, sweet, Lydia without whom none of the events of the past twenty-four hours would ever have happened. Abigail wasn't sure whether she wanted to hug her or stay angry at her for locking her up.

Looking towards her desk she saw a rather round man sitting in her chair. Deciding that she'd get to him in a minute, Abigail took Wanda and locked her in the jail cell. It was only after doing so, that she noticed the last person in the room. Maggie. *Maggie!*

"Oh my gosh! Maggie, is it really you?" Abigail quickly went to give her cousin a welcoming hug.

"Yes, it's me. I just arrived and was surprised to find the entire town in some sort of an uproar which involved you, a crime and a man." Laughing, she returned Abigail's hug with exuberance.

The man sitting in her chair cleared his throat, interrupting their reunion.

"Excuse me, Sheriff. But I believe we have some business to take care of."

Still unaware of exactly who this man was, Abigail released her cousin and, walking to her desk, said, "I don't believe we've met."

"I'm Walter McCurdy, the circuit court judge. I'm here about one Mr. Cole Stanton." Consulting a sheaf of papers that he'd laid on the desk in front of him, he recited, "Cole Stanton wanted for jewel theft in the city of Albany, New York. Apprehended in the town of Surprise, New York, awaiting trial in said town." Glancing up, he asked, "Did I leave anything out?"

Did he leave anything out? Abigail was stunned as she was sure were most of the others in the room. Looking back and forth from Wanda to the judge it was easy to see the family resemblance. Why was he acting as if he didn't recognize the woman behind bars?

"In the short time I've been in Surprise, though, it seems that Mr. Stanton's lot may have changed."

"Yes. A short time ago I arrested Wanda *Mc-Curdy*." Even after emphasizing the last name, the man didn't flinch. He was pointedly ignoring the woman in jail. "Mr. Stanton is innocent of the charges brought against him. Miss McCurdy has admitted to committing the crime. Perhaps, you sir, could enlighten me as to why she would do such a thing?"

Looking right into her eyes, he said, "I could, but I don't know why my daughter robs and steals."

"I do it so you'll remember who I am. I'm your daughter, your only daughter whom you choose to ignore." Sobbing, Wanda sat down in the bunk with her head resting in her hands.

"Perhaps you could leave us alone for a moment." Walter McCurdy lifted his bulk from the chair.

Abigail nodded and followed Lydia and Maggie outside. The town had settled into the morning routine. Aunt Margaret sat in her wheelchair like a sentinel standing guard or, in her case, sitting guard. Cole sat on the stoop talking to her. They both looked up as the three women exited the office.

"I must say Miss Margaret that you have the loveliest nieces," Cole drawled. "There's one in particular though who strikes my fancy."

Abigail felt herself blushing, the warmth spreading from her neck up to her cheeks.

Rising from the step, he reached out and took her hand in his. "If you ladies will excuse us, I believe that the Sheriff and I have some unfinished business."

"Take your time. Maggie and Lydia can take me home. I feel the need for some honey-laced tea."

"I can't leave the McCurdys alone . . ." Abigail began to protest.

Margaret waved a hand in the air. "John will see to them. You run along with your young man."

Abigail was about to scold her aunt for interfering in her job once again, but Cole shot her a warning look. Instead, she agreed to let Mr. Wagner entertain the McCurdy family until she was finished with her business.

"If you're interested, I know a place where we can talk uninterrupted." Cole gave her a wicked smile.

Chapter Eighteen

Her heart fluttered. "I'm interested."

Taking the path that led around to the back of the buildings, he took her to the very spot where she'd first shot a gun. The sunlight-dappled shade of the big oak tree spread around them like a blanket. Abigail hadn't really taken the time to come back here since that day. Surprisingly enough, her days had been filled with the duties of being the town's sheriff.

And she realized those same days had been filled with Cole Stanton. The same man who stood before her now, wearing the same intense look on his face, she remembered from the first day they'd met. The way those dark, dark eyes were looking at her right now made her heartbeat trip at a faster pace, and it felt as if butterflies were alighting in her stomach. A shivery feeling of delight slid down her spine.

"You are so beautiful." He spoke the words, slowly, softly, words meant only for her to hear.

She swallowed. "And you are the most handsome man I've ever known."

"I didn't say that so you'd return the favor."

"I know."

Running a finger along her jaw-line, Cole continued to stare at her, and it was then that she caught the look. It was as if he wanted to memorize her features. Her heart tripped along, only this time it was with a feeling of dread. She wanted to hold him close and never let him go. Abigail knew her life would never be the same if he left.

"Are you leaving?"

His face was inches from hers, so she saw the look of surprise in his eyes. Tears sprung to her eyes. A sob rose in her chest.

"Please, don't cry." His voice was husky with emotion.

She wanted to scream at him, to pummel his chest with her hands. How could he dare to take her heart and then hand it back to her? He was going to leave, to move on, to become a drifter once more, and she had to somehow find a way to stop him, to make him stay.

"Aunt Margaret will be very upset with you if you leave Surprise."

"What?"

Pushing away from him she continued, "My aunt has invested a lot of time and energy pursuing you."

"Your aunt has nothing to do with this." With his hands placed firmly on his hips and standing at his full height, Cole reminded her of the man she'd met that night in the saloon so many weeks ago.

He looked surly and every bit like a bear, except with his beard gone, she was able to clearly see the expressions on his face. Cole may not know it, but right now he was looking every bit bemused. She had him right where she wanted him. And just where was that? Abigail wondered.

Running his hands through his thick hair, he looked at her standing so bravely before him. "Abby. How can I make you understand?"

"I love you."

The words were carried to him on a warm breeze, and for a moment he let his heart swell. He couldn't remember the last time someone had told him they loved him.

"Don't you understand, I could never let you go."

"You don't have to let me go, Cole. All you have to do is let me into your heart." Taking a few tentative steps towards him, Abigail looked at him.

He'd have to be blind not to see the love shining in her eyes.

"It's not that simple."

"Yes, it is."

Abigail was inches from him. He could feel the heat from her body penetrating his clothing.

"You have to remember what I told you last night. It's time for you to let go, Cole Stanton. It's time for you to love and be loved again. Tell me why you were smiling when I awoke this morning?"

With the excitement of their morning escapades, he'd almost forgotten about the dream. "Last night was the first time I'd ever had a good dream about my sister. We were sitting under the apple tree in the backyard and Beth was handing me apples, big red ones. She was smiling and laughing. Abby, it was the first time I hadn't seen her dying."

Rushing into his arms, she gathered him close. "Oh, Cole, don't you see, it's a sign from heaven. Beth is telling you to be happy."

Sobs began to rack his body. He held on tightly to Abigail. She began running her hands lightly up and down his spine, soothing him.

"Let go of your sorrow, Cole. I promise you your life will be better from now on."

Cupping her face between his hands, he lowered his mouth to hers. Through the tears they kissed each other.

"I love you, Abigail Monroe. With all my heart and my soul, I love you."

A smattering of applause erupted. Abigail and

Cole spun around to find Maggie, Lydia, Mr. Wagner and Aunt Margaret smiling back at them.

"It's about time you two came to your senses." Aunt Margaret beamed and clapped her hands together delightedly.

"Miss Margaret, you and I need to have a few words." Without waiting for a reply, Cole strode over to her and, grabbing the handles of the wheelchair, pushed her over to the oak tree.

Leaning against the fence railing, Cole crossed his arms over his chest, and his feet at the ankles.

"You know my secret, don't you?"

He nodded. "Uh-huh. I knew it from the first time I had dinner at your home."

"How come you haven't told my girls?"

While he pretended to ponder the question, Miss Margaret shifted uncomfortably in her seat.

"I imagine Abigail would have my head if I ever said anything bad about you, Miss Margaret."

With a twinkle in her eye, she stated, "I see she already has your heart."

"Yes, ma'am, she does."

"Push me back to my family, Mr. Stanton. We've a wedding to plan."

Wedding! Why he'd only just declared his love for Abigail! Taking hold of the handles once more, he pushed her along the dirt to where the girls stood in a semi-circle. "You should know I haven't proposed to her."

"I'll just have to fix that, now won't I?"

Pulling the chair to a stop in the middle of the yard, he walked around and knelt in front of Margaret Monroe Sinclair, the grand dame of Surprise. "Here's the deal; I won't tell your nieces you've been faking this illness, and in return you're going to let me propose to Abigail on my own."

For a moment she looked stricken at the idea of her little secret coming out, and then with a regal nod of her head she agreed to his terms.

Two days later Cole walked into the sheriff's office a free man. Wanda McCurdy had returned to Albany accompanied by her father and a marshal. He'd heard that the items she'd stolen had been returned and she'd been sentenced to six months in the city jail.

He felt sorry for her, but if not for Wanda he never would have found out how much he needed Abigail, so for that he owed her.

"I kind of miss being your prisoner."

Abigail looked up from the paperwork she'd been tending to and smiled at him. "Hello."

Dropping a kiss on her forehead, he sat down on the edge of her desk. "Hello, yourself. Do you think you could finish this work another time?"

"Well now it depends on whether or not I'm going to get a better offer."

He loved it when she bantered with him. "I guess you're going to have to trust me."

"I'll always trust you, Cole."

Wiggling his eyebrows at her, Cole helped her up from the desk. "I have a surprise for you."

Feigning innocence, she pressed her hand dramatically to her chest. "For me, you have a surprise for little ol' me?"

"I'm calling it 'A Surprise for Abigail!' "

"I like the sound of that." With complete faith and trust she walked with Cole down the street. "Where are we going?"

"To the schoolhouse."

"Cole, I finished my studies a long, long time ago."

"I know. I've something to show you."

The smell of fresh-cut lumber and freshly painted siding filled the air. Abigail liked the smell, it meant Surprise was alive. Pushing open the tall doors, Cole led her into the classroom.

Abigail looked around in wonder. Three long windows lined either side of the outside walls. She could see the large square space in the front of the room where the chalkboards were to be installed. The wideboard pine floors had been swept clean of sawdust.

"This is lovely."

"I wanted you to be the first to see what I've been

doing every day." Stepping away from her, he flung his arms wide. "All of this lumber came from Alexander Judson's place. Don't you just love the smell of fresh-cut lumber."

His enthusiasm was contagious and Abigail smiled back at him, laughing in delight.

"In case I haven't told you lately, I love you."

Her smile broadened. "I know."

Suddenly he turned from her and went behind the new teacher's desk to retrieve something. Straightening, Cole held a beautiful bunch of wildflowers. Walking to her, he handed her the bouquet. She buried her nose in the brilliant colors, the smell was so sweet. Before she knew what he was about, Cole was before her on bended knee.

Taking her hand in his, he looked deeply into her eyes. "Abigail Monroe, will you marry me?"

"Yes, Cole Stanton. Yes!" Heedless of the flowers clutched in her hands, she knelt before him and embraced him, crushing the petals on his back. "I love you."

Their lips met in the sweetest of kisses. Abigail knew every time she smelled flowers like these, they would forever remind her of this moment.

Nuzzling her head against his neck she said, "I think I could learn to love your surprises."

"You know what the biggest one of all was?"

She shook her head.

"Our finding each other and falling in love. Oh,

Abby, I thought my life was over and then I met you and everything changed."

"I'm glad you drifted into my town."

Chuckling, he said, "Me, too, Sheriff. Me too."